"Allow me?" he asked, reaching for the bow on her faux fur stole.

Ophelia gave him a quiet nod as he tugged on the end of the satin ribbon. He loosened the bow and opened the stole a bit. Just enough to offer a glimpse of the spectacular diamonds around her neck.

"There," he said. "That's better."

Ophelia swallowed, unable to move, unable to even breathe while he touched her. She'd dropped her guard. Only for a moment. And now...

Now he was no more than a breath away, and she could see her reflection in the cool gray of his irises. He had eyes like a tempest, and there she was, right at the center of his storm. Looking beautiful and happy. Full of life and hope. So much like her old self, the old Ophelia—the girl who'd danced through life, unfettered and unafraid—that she forgot all the reasons why she shouldn't kiss this man. This man who had such a way of reminding her who she used to be.

"I'm sorry." She removed her hand from Artem's face and slid across the leather seat, out of his reach "I shouldn't have... I'm sorry."

"Ophelia," he said with more patience in his tone than she'd ever heard. "It's okay."

But it wasn't okay. *She* wasn't okay.

"Showtime," he muttered.

Showtime.

DRAKE DIAMONDS: Looking for love that shines as bright as the gems in their window!

Dear Reader,

Welcome to the glamorous world of Drake Diamonds on Fifth Avenue in snowy New York City! *His Ballerina Bride* is the first book in my debut series for Harlequin Special Edition, and I couldn't be more excited to share this story.

Former ballerina Ophelia Rose is reeling from a medical diagnosis that has turned her life upside down. Forced to retire from the stage, she's heartbroken at the prospect of an uncertain and lonely future. But then she meets her new boss, Artem Drake, the reluctant head of a family diamond empire, and he seems determined to show her that nothing is quite as precious as a glittering new beginning.

So many things inspired Ophelia and Artem's story— my love of ballet, the glitz and glamour of New York and, of course, a fondness for Audrey Hepburn in *Breakfast at Tiffany's*. It might be the most romantic book I've ever written. It's definitely the first one to feature a kitten instead of a dog. This one's for you, cat lovers! I hope you have as much fun reading it as I did putting the words on the pages.

Happy reading,

Teri Wilson

His Ballerina Bride

Teri Wilson

HARLEQUIN® SPECIAL EDITION®

Recycling programs
for this product may
not exist in your area.

ISBN-13: 978-0-373-62325-9

His Ballerina Bride

Printed in U.S.A.

Teri Wilson is a novelist for Harlequin Books. She is the author of *Unleashing Mr. Darcy*, now a Hallmark Channel Original Movie. Teri is also a contributing writer at HelloGiggles.com, a lifestyle and entertainment website founded by Zooey Deschanel that is now part of the *People* magazine, *TIME* magazine and *Entertainment Weekly* family. Teri loves books, travel, animals and dancing every day. Visit Teri at www.teriwilson.net or on Twitter, @TeriWilsonauthr.

Books by Teri Wilson

HQN Books

Unmasking Juliet
Unleashing Mr. Darcy

Visit the Author Profile page
at Harlequin.com for more titles.

For the classic-movie lovers out there
who dream of little black dresses, diamonds
and breakfast on Fifth Avenue.

"People will stare. Make it worth their while."

—Harry Winston

Chapter One

They say diamonds are a girl's best friend. Ophelia Rose had a tendency to disagree. Strongly.

Not that Ophelia had anything against diamonds per se. On the contrary, she adored them. Just two months ago, she'd earned an entire college degree in diamonds. Gemology, technically. Every piece of jewelry she'd designed for her final independent study project featured a diamond as its centerpiece. They were something of a pet jewel of hers. So naturally, working at Drake Diamonds was her dream job. It was her dream job *now*, anyway. Now that all vestiges of her former life had pretty much vanished.

Now that she'd been forced to start over.

She still loved diamonds. In truth, only *certain* diamonds had been getting on her nerves of late. Diamonds of the engagement variety. The level of stress that those particular gems were causing her was enough to make her seriously question their best-friend status. Unfortunately, engagement diamonds were something of an occupational hazard for someone who worked on the tenth floor of Drake Diamonds.

Ophelia pasted on a smile and focused on the glittering jewels in the display case before her and the way they dazzled beneath the radiant store lights. *Breathe. Just breathe.*

"This is the one. Princess cut. It's perfect for you…" The man sitting across from Ophelia slipped a 2.3-carat solitaire onto the ring finger of the woman sitting beside him and cooed, "…princess."

"Oh, stop. You're going to make me cry again," his fiancée said, gazing at the diamond on her hand. Sure enough, a lone tear slipped down her cheek.

Ophelia slid a box of rose-scented tissues toward the princess.

In the course of a typical workday, Ophelia went through at least two boxes of tissues. Twice that many on the weekend, along with countless flutes of the finest French champagne and dozens of delicate petits fours crafted to look like the distinctive Drake Diamonds blue gift box crowned with its signature white ribbon. Because shopping for an engagement ring at Drake Diamonds was an experience steeped in luxury, as it had been since 1830.

Her current customers couldn't have cared less about the trappings, particularly the edible ones. Their champagne flutes were nearly full and the petits fours completely untouched. Ophelia was fairly certain the only things they wanted to consume were each other.

It made her heart absolutely ache.

Six months had passed since Ophelia's diagnosis. She'd had half a year to accept her fate, half a year to come to terms with her new reality. She'd never be the girl with the diamond on her finger. She'd never be the bride-to-be. Multiple sclerosis was a serious, chronic illness, one that had altered every aspect of her existence. It had been difficult enough to let this uninvited guest turn her life upside down. She wouldn't let it do the same to someone else. That much she could control.

She couldn't dictate a lot of things about her new life. But her single status was one of them. And she was perfectly fine with it. She had enough on her plate with work, volunteering at the animal shelter and staying as healthy as possible. Not to mention coping with everything she'd left behind.

Still.

Being reminded on a daily basis of what she would never have was getting old.

"Look at that. It's a perfect fit." She smiled at the happy couple, and her throat grew tight. "Shall I wrap it for you?"

"Yes, please." The besotted man's gaze never left his betrothed. "In one of those fancy blue boxes?"

Ophelia nodded. "Of course. It's my pleasure."

She gathered the ring and the petits fours—which the bride declared were in flagrant violation of her wedding diet—and padded across the plush blue carpet of the sales floor toward the gift-wrap room. After dropping off the diamond ring, where it would be boxed, wrapped and tied with a bridal-white bow, she made her way to the kitchen to dispose of the tiny cakes.

She stopped and stared at the counter and the endless rows of pristine silver plates and champagne flutes. Once her current customers left, she'd be passing out another pair of fancy desserts. Another duo of champagne glasses. To yet another couple madly in love.

I can't keep doing this.

This wasn't the plan. The plan was to work in jewelry design, to sketch and create the pieces in those glittering display cases. Catering to the lovesick was definitely *not* the plan.

She knew she should be grateful. She had to start somewhere. As far as the sales team went, working on the tenth floor in Engagements was the most coveted position in the building. She simply needed to bide her time until she could somehow show upper management what she could do, and get transferred to the design department.

One day at a time. I can do this.

She could totally do it. But maybe all those happily engaged couples would be easier to stomach with a little cake.

Why not? No one was looking. Everyone was on the sales floor.

Ophelia had never been much of a rule breaker. She'd never broken *any* rules, come to think of it. Funny how being the good girl all her life hadn't stopped her world from falling apart. Life wasn't fair. She should have known that by now.

She closed her eyes and bit into one of the petits fours. As it melted in her mouth, she contemplated the healing powers of sugar and frosting. Cake might not be the best thing for the body, but at the moment, it was doing wonders for her battered soul.

Finally, she'd uncovered the one good thing about no longer being a professional ballet dancer. Cake. She couldn't remember the last time she'd had a bite of the sweet dessert. Not even on her birthday.

"My God, where have you been all my life?" she whispered.

"Excuse my tardiness," a sultry male voice said in return.

Oh, God.

Ophelia's eyes flew open.

Much to her dismay, the bemused retort hadn't come from the petit four. It had come from her boss. Artem Drake, in the flesh. His tuxedo-clad, playboy flesh.

"Mr. Drake." Her throat grew tight.

What was he even doing here? No one at Drake Diamonds had laid eyes on him since he'd inherited the company from his father. Unless the photos of him on *Page Six* counted.

And good grief. He was a thousand times hotter in person than he was on the internet. How was that even possible?

Ophelia took in his square chin, his dark, knowing gaze and the hint of a dimple in his left cheek, and went a little bit weak in the knees. The fit of his tuxedo was impeccable. As was the shine of his patent leather shoes. But it was the look on his face that nearly did her in. Like the cat who got the cream.

The man was decadence personified.

She swallowed. With great difficulty. "This isn't what it looks like."

She couldn't be seen eating one of the Drake petits fours. They were for customers, not employees. Not to mention the mortification of being caught moaning suggestively at a baked good. She dropped it like a hot potato. It landed between them on the kitchen floor with a splat. A crumb bounced onto the mirror surface of one of Artem's shoes.

What on *earth* was she doing?

He glanced down and lifted a provocative brow. Ophelia's insides went all fluttery. Perfect. She'd already made an idiot of herself and now she was borderline swooning over an eyebrow. Her *boss's* eyebrow.

"Oh, good," he said, his deep voice heavily laced with amusement. "Thanks for clearing that up. For a minute, I thought I'd stumbled upon one of my employees eating the custom-made, fifteen-dollars-per-square-inch snacks that we serve our customers."

Those petits fours were fifteen dollars apiece? That seemed insane, even for Drake Diamonds. They were good, but they weren't that good.

Ophelia glanced at the tiny cake at her feet, and her stomach growled. Okay, maybe they were that good. "Um…"

"So what's the story, then? Are you a runaway fiancée hiding in my kitchen?" His gaze flitted to the floor again. "Are those pretty feet of yours getting cold?"

"A fiancée? Me? No. Definitely not." Once upon a time, yes. But that, like so many other things, had changed. "I mean, no. Just…no."

Stop talking. She was making things so much worse, but she couldn't seem to think straight.

Those pretty feet of yours…

"So you do work for me, then?" He crossed his arms and leaned against the kitchen counter, the perfect picture of elegant nonchalance.

What was he doing, wearing a tux at ten in the morning, anyway? On a weekday, no less. Was this some kind of billionaire walk of shame?

Probably. She thought about the countless photos she'd seen of him with young, beautiful women on his arm. Sometimes two or three at a time. *Walk of shame. Definitely.*

"I do," she said. I do. *I do.* Wedding words. Her neck went instantly, unbearably hot. She cleared her throat. "I work in Engagements."

The corner of his lips twitched. So he thought that was funny, did he? "And your name is?"

"Ophelia." She paused. "Ophelia Rose." At least she had her wits about her enough to identify herself by her actual, real last name and not the stage name she'd been using for the last eight years. Out of everything in her life that had changed, no longer calling herself Ophelia Baronova had been the most difficult to accept. As if that person really, truly no longer existed.

She doesn't.

Ophelia bit her lower lip to keep it from trembling.

Artem Drake crossed his arms. "I suppose that makes me your boss."

This was getting weird.

"Come now, Ophelia Rose. Don't look so sad. I'm not going to fire you for biting into temptation." One corner of Mr. Drake's perfect mouth lifted into a half grin. "Literally."

Clearly, he knew a thing or two about temptation. How was it possible for a man to so fully embody sex?

"Good." She forced a smile. Being fired hadn't actually crossed her mind, although she supposed it should have. It was just kind of difficult to take Artem seriously, since he hadn't darkened the door of Drake Diamonds in the entire time she'd worked there. But if he thought the sadness behind her eyes was because she was afraid of him, so be it. That was fine. Better, actually. She wasn't about to bare her messed-up soul to her employer.

Her employer...

When would she have another opportunity to talk to Artem Drake one-on-one? Never, probably. Because she sure wasn't planning on sneaking off to the kitchen anymore. And who knew when he'd show up again? She had to make the most of this moment. If she didn't, she'd regret it. Just as soon as she went back out on the sales floor among all those engaged couples.

It was now or never.

But maybe she should scrape the cake off the floor first.

Artem Drake was having difficulty wrapping his mind around the fact that the goddess of a woman who'd just dropped to her knees in front of him worked for him. But to be fair, the concept of anyone in this Fifth Avenue institution answering to him was somewhat laughable.

Granted, his last name was on the front of the building. And the gift bags. And those legendary blue boxes. But he'd never had much to do with running the place. That had been his father's job. And now that his father was gone, the responsibility should fall on the shoulders of his older brother, Dalton. Dalton lived and breathed Drake Diamonds. Dalton spent so much time here that he had a foldout sofa in his office. Hell, Artem didn't even *have* an office.

Nor did he have any idea how much those silly little cakes cost. He'd pulled a number out of thin air. And now he'd nearly made the goddess cry. Maybe he was cut out to run the place, after all. His dad had loved making people cry.

Besides, *goddess* wasn't quite the right word. There was something ethereal about her. Delicate. Unspeakably graceful. She had a neck made for diamonds.

Which sounded exactly like something his father would say.

"Stand up," Artem said, far more harshly than he'd intended. But if she didn't get up off her knees, he wouldn't have any hope of maintaining an ounce of professional behavior.

She finished dabbing at the mess with a napkin and stood, her motions so effortlessly fluid that the air around her seemed to dance. "Yes, sir."

He rather liked the *sir* business. But he needed to do

what he'd come here to do and get the hell out of this place. He pushed away from the counter and straightened his cuff link. Singular. One of them had managed to go missing since the symphony gala the night before. Maybe he'd pick up a new pair on his way out. *After* he'd waved the proverbial white flag in his brother's face.

He cleared his throat. "While this has been interesting, to say the least, I have some business to attend to. And I'm sure you have work to do, as well."

Could he sound more ridiculous? *I have some business to attend to. And I'm sure you have work to do, as well.* He'd never spoken like that in his life. Dalton, yes. All the time. That's probably how he spoke to his girlfriends.

"Wait," Ophelia blurted, just as he took a step toward the door. "Please, Mr. Drake. Sir."

He turned. "Yes, Miss Rose?"

"I'd like to schedule a meeting with you. At your convenience, of course." She lifted her chin, and her neck seemed to lengthen.

God, that neck. Artem let his gaze travel down the length of it to the delicate dip between her collarbones. A diamond would look exquisite nestled right there, set off by her perfect porcelain skin. Artem had never seen such a beautiful complexion on a woman. She almost looked as though she'd never set foot outdoors. Like she was crafted of the purest, palest marble. Like she belonged in a museum rather than here. What in God's name was she doing working behind a jewelry counter, anyway?

He lifted his gaze back to her face, and her cheeks went rosebud pink. "A meeting? With me?"

He'd heard worse ideas.

"Yes. A business meeting," she said crisply. "I have some design ideas I'd like to present. I know I work in sales at the moment, but I'm actually a trained gemologist."

Artem wasn't sure why he found this news so surprising, but he did. Few people surprised him. He wished more of them did. Ophelia Rose was becoming more intriguing by the minute.

She was also his *employee*, at least for the next ten minutes or so. He shouldn't be thinking about her neck. Or the soft swell of her breasts beneath the bodice of the vintage sea-foam dress she wore. Or what her delicate bottom would feel like in the palms of his hands. He shouldn't be thinking about any of the images that were currently running through his mind.

"A gemologist? Really?" he said, somehow keeping his gaze fixed on her face. God, he deserved a medal for such restraint.

She nodded. "I've have a degree from the New York School of Design. I graduated with honors."

"Then congratulations are in order. Perhaps even a celebration." He just couldn't help himself. "With cake."

Her blush deepened a shade closer to crimson. "Honestly, I'd rather have that meeting. Just half an hour of your time to show you my designs. That's all I need."

She was determined. He'd give her that. Determined and oh-so-earnest.

And rather bold, now that he thought about it. He

had, after all, just walked in on her shoving cake in her mouth. Cake meant for lovebirds prepared to drop thousands of dollars for a Drake diamond. She had a ballsy streak. Sexy, he mused.

Artem wondered how much he was paying her. He hadn't a clue. "I'm sorry, but I can't."

She took a step closer to him, and he caught a whiff of something warm and sweet. Vanilla maybe. She smelled like a dessert, which Artem supposed made perfect sense. "Can't or won't?"

He shrugged. "I guess you could say both."

She opened her lovely mouth to protest, and Artem held up a hand to stop her. "Miss Rose, before you waste any more of your precious time, there's something you should know. I'm resigning."

She went quiet for a beat. A beat during which Artem wondered what had prompted him to tell this total stranger his plans before he'd even discussed them with his own flesh and blood. He blamed it on his hangover. Or possibly the sad, haunted look in Ophelia's blue eyes. Eyes the color of Kashmir sapphires.

It didn't seem right to let her think he could help her when he'd never even see her again.

"Resigning?" She frowned. "But you can't resign. This is Drake Diamonds, and you're a Drake."

Not the right Drake. "I'm quitting my family business, not my family." Although the thought wasn't without its merits, considering he'd never truly been one of them. Not the way Dalton and their sister, Diana, had.

"But your father left you in charge." Her voice had gone as soft as feathers. *Feathers.* A bird. That's what she reminded him of—a swan. A stunning, sylphlike swan. "That matters."

He shook his head. She had no clue what she was talking about, and he wasn't about to elaborate. He'd already said too much. And frankly, it was none of her business. "I assure you, this is for the best. I might add that it's also confidential."

"Oh, I won't tell anyone."

"I know you won't." He pointed at the petit four that she'd scraped up off the floor, still resting in her palm. "You'll keep my secret, and I'll keep yours. Does that sound fair, princess?"

His news wouldn't be a secret for long, anyway. Dalton's office was right down the hall. If Artem hadn't heard Ophelia's sensual ode to cake and made this spontaneous detour, the deed would already be done.

He'd enjoyed toying with her, but now their encounter had taken a rather vexing turn. As much as he liked the thought of half an hour behind closed doors with those lithe limbs and willowy grace, the meeting she so desperately wanted simply wasn't going to happen. Not with him, anyway.

Maybe Dalton would meet with her. Maybe Artem would suggest it. *I quit. Oh, and by the way, one of the sales associates wants to design our next collection...*

Maybe not.

"Okay, then. It was nice meeting you, Mr. Drake." She offered him her free hand, and he took it. "I'm so very sorry for your loss."

That last part came out as little more than a whisper, just breathy enough for Artem to know that Ophelia

Rose with the sad sapphire eyes knew a little something about loss herself.

"Thank you." Her hand felt small in his. Small and impossibly soft.

Then she withdrew her hand and squared her shoulders, and the fleeting glimpse of vulnerability he'd witnessed was replaced with the cool confidence of a woman who'd practically thrown cake at him and then asked for a meeting to discuss a promotion. There was that ballsy streak again. "One last thing, Mr. Drake."

He suppressed a grin. "Yes?"

"Don't call me princess."

Chapter Two

"Really, Artem?" Dalton aimed a scandalized glance at Artem's unbuttoned collar and loosened bow tie. "That penthouse where you live is less than three blocks away. You couldn't be bothered to go home and change before coming to work?"

Artem shrugged and sank into one of the ebony wing chairs opposite Dalton desk. "Don't push it. I'm here, aren't I?"

Present and accounted for. Physically, at least. His thoughts, along with his libido, still lingered back in the kitchen with the intriguing Miss Rose.

"At long last. It's been two months since Dad died. To what do we owe the honor of your presence?" Dalton twirled his pen, a Montblanc. Just like the one their father had always used. It could have been the same one, for all Artem knew. That would have been an appropriate bequest.

Far more appropriate than leaving Artem in charge of this place when he'd done nothing more than pass out checks and attend charity galas since he'd been on the payroll.

The only Drake who spent less time in the building than he did was their sister, Diana. She was busy training for the Olympic equestrian team with her horse, which was appropriately named Diamond.

Artem narrowed his gaze at his brother. "I've been busy."

"Busy," Dalton said flatly. "Right. I think I remember reading something about that in *Page Six*."

"And here I thought you only read the financial pages. Don't tell me you've lowered yourself to reading *Page Six*, brother."

"I have to, don't I? How else would I keep apprised of your whereabouts?" The smile on Dalton's face grew tight.

A dull ache throbbed to life in Artem's temples, and he remembered why he'd put off this meeting for as long as he had. It wasn't as if he and Dalton had ever been close, but at least they'd managed to be cordial to one another while their father was alive. Now it appeared the gloves were off.

The thing was, he sympathized with Dalton. Surely his older brother had expected to be next in line to run the company. Hell, everyone had expected that to be the case.

He didn't feel too sorry for Dalton, though. He was

about to get exactly what he wanted. Besides, Artem would *not* let Dalton ruin his mood. He'd had a pleasant enough evening at the symphony gala, which had led to a rather sexually satisfying morning.

Oddly enough, though, it had been the unexpected encounter with Ophelia Rose that had put the spring in his step.

He found her interesting. And quite lovely. She would have made it almost tolerable to come to work every day, if he had any intention of doing such a thing. Which he didn't.

"Has it occurred to you that having the Drake name in the papers is good PR?" Artem said blithely.

"PR. Is that what they're calling it nowadays?" Dalton rolled his eyes.

It took every ounce of Artem's self-restraint not to point out how badly his brother needed to get laid. "I didn't come here to discuss my social life, Dalton. As difficult as you might find it to believe, I'm ready to discuss business."

Dalton nodded. Slowly. "I'm glad to hear that, brother. Very glad."

He'd be even happier once Artem made his announcement. So would Artem. He had no desire to engage in this sort of exchange on a daily basis. He was a grown man. He didn't need his brother's input on his lifestyle. And he sure as hell didn't want to sit behind a desk all day at a place where he'd never been welcomed when his father had been alive.

According to the attorneys, his father had changed the provisions of his will less than a week before he'd died. One might suppose senility to be behind the change, if not for the fact that his dad had been too stubborn to lose his mind. Shrewd. Cold. And sharp as a tack until the day he passed.

"Listen," Artem said. "I don't know why Dad left me in charge. It's as much of a mystery to me as it is to you."

"Don't." Dalton shook his head. "It doesn't matter. What's done is done. You're here. That's a start. I've had Dad's office cleaned out. It's yours now."

Artem went still. "What?"

Dalton shrugged one shoulder. "Where else are you going to work?"

Artem didn't have an answer for that.

Dalton continued, "Listen, it's going to take a few days to get you up to speed. We have one pressing matter, though, that just can't wait. If you hadn't rolled in here by the end of the week, I was going to beat down your door at the Plaza and insist you talk to me."

Whatever the pressing matter was, Artem had a feeling that he didn't want to hear about it. He didn't need to. It wasn't his problem. This idea that he would actually run the company was a joke.

"Before the heart attack…" Dalton's voice lost a bit of its edge.

The change in his composure was barely perceptible, but Artem noticed. He'd actually expected his brother to be more of a mess. Dalton, after all, had been the jewel in their father's crown. He'd been a son, whereas Artem had been a stranger to the Drakes for the first five years of his life.

"…Dad invested in a new mine in Australia. I didn't even know about it until last week." Dalton raised his brows, as if Artem had something to say.

Artem let out a laugh. "Surely you're not suggesting that he told *me* about it."

His brother sighed. "I suppose not, although I wish he had. I wish someone had stopped him. It doesn't matter, anyway. What's done is done. The mine was a bust. It's worthless, and now it's put the business in a rather precarious position."

"Precarious? Exactly how much did he spend on this mine?"

Dalton took too long to answer. He exhaled a slow, measured breath and finally said, "Three billion."

"Three billion dollars." Artem blinked. That was a lot of money. An astronomical amount, even to a man who lived on the eighteenth floor of the Plaza and flew his own Boeing business jet, which, ironically enough, Artem used for pleasure far more than he did for business. "The company has billions in assets, though. If not trillions."

"Yes, but not all those assets are liquid. With the loss from the mine, we're sitting at a twenty-five million dollar deficit. We need to figure something out."

We. Since when did any of the Drakes consider Artem part of a *we*?

He should just get up and walk right out of Dalton's office. He didn't owe the Drakes a thing.

Somehow, though, his backside remained rooted to the spot. "What about the diamond?"

"*The* diamond? The *Drake* diamond?" Dalton shook

his head. "I'm going to pretend I didn't hear that. I know you're not one for sentimentality, brother, but even you wouldn't suggest that we sell the Drake diamond."

Actually, he would. "It's a rock, Dalton. A pretty rock, but a rock nonetheless."

Dalton shook his head so hard that Artem thought it might snap clear off his neck. "It's a piece of history. Our family name was built on that rock."

Our family name. Right.

Artem cleared his throat. "How much is it worth?"

"It doesn't matter, because we're not selling it."

"How much, Dalton? As your superior, I demand that you tell me." It was a low blow. Artem would have liked to think that a small part of him didn't get a perverse sort of pleasure from throwing his position in Dalton's face, but it did. So be it.

"Fifty million dollars," Dalton said. "But I repeat, it's not for sale, and it never will be."

Never.

If Artem had learned one thing since becoming acquainted with his father—since being "welcomed" into the Drake fold—it was that *never* was an awfully strong word. "That's not your call, though, is it, brother?"

Ophelia hadn't planned on stopping by the animal shelter on the way home from work. She had, after all, already volunteered three times this week. Possibly four. She'd lost count.

She couldn't go home yet, though. Not after the day she'd had. Dealing with all the happily engaged couples was bad enough, but she was growing accustomed to it. She didn't have much of a choice, did she? But the unexpected encounter with Artem Drake had somehow thrown her completely off-kilter.

It wasn't only the embarrassment of getting caught inhaling one of the fifteen dollar petits fours that had gotten her so rattled. It was him. Artem.

Mr. Drake. Not Artem. *He's your boss, not your friend. Or anything else.*

He wasn't even her boss anymore, she supposed. Which was for the best. Obviously. She hadn't exactly made a glowing first impression. Now she could start over with whoever took his place. So really, there was no logical reason for the acute tug of disappointment she'd felt when he'd told her about his plans to resign. None whatsoever.

There was also no logical reason that she'd kept looking around all afternoon for a glimpse of him as he exited the building. Nor for the way she'd gone all fluttery when she'd caught a flash of tuxedoed pant leg beyond the closing elevator doors after her shift had ended. It hadn't been Artem, anyway. Just another, less dashing man dressed to the nines.

What was her problem, anyway? She was acting as though she'd never met a handsome man before. Artem Drake wasn't merely handsome, though. He was charming.

Too charming. Dangerously so.

Ophelia had felt uncharacteristically vulnerable in the presence of all that charm. Raw. Empty. And acutely aware of all that she'd lost, all that she'd never have.

She couldn't go home to the apartment she'd inherited from her grandmother. She couldn't spend another evening sifting through her grandmother's things—the grainy black-and-white photographs, her tattered pointe shoes. Her grandmother had been the only family that Ophelia had known since the tender age of two, when a car accident claimed the lives of her parents. Natalia Baronova had been more than a grandparent. She'd been Ophelia's world. Her mother figure, her best friend and her ballet teacher.

She'd died a week before Ophelia's diagnosis. As much as Ophelia had needed someone to lean on in those first dark days, she'd been grateful that the great Natalia Baronova, star ballerina of Ballet Russe de Monte Carlo in the 1940s and '50s, died without the knowledge that her beloved granddaughter would never dance again.

"Ophelia?" Beth, the shelter manager, shook her head and planted her hands on her hips as Ophelia slipped off her coat and hung it on one of the pegs by the door. "Again? I didn't see your name on the volunteer schedule for this evening."

"It's not. But I thought you could use an extra pair of hands." Ophelia flipped through the notebook that contained the animals' daily feeding schedule.

"You know better than anybody we always need help around here, but surely you have somewhere else to be on a Friday night."

Nowhere, actually. "You know how much I enjoy spending time with the animals." Plus, the shelter was now caring for a litter of eight three-week-old kittens that had to be bottle-fed every three hours. The skimpy volunteer staff could barely keep up, especially now that the city was blanketed with snow. People liked to stay home when it snowed. And that meant at any given moment, one of the kittens was hungry.

Beth nodded. "I know, love. Just be careful. I'd hate for you to ruin that pretty dress you're wearing."

The dress had belonged to Ophelia's grandmother. In addition to mountains of dance memorabilia, she'd left behind a gorgeous collection of vintage clothing. Like the apartment, it had been a godsend. When she'd been dancing, Ophelia had lived in a leotard and tights. Most days, she'd even worn her dance clothes to school, since she'd typically had to go straight from rehearsal to class at the New York School of Design. She couldn't very well show up to work at Drake Diamonds dressed in a wraparound sweater, pink tights and leg warmers.

Neither could she simply go out and buy a whole new work wardrobe. Between her student loan bills and the exorbitant cost of the biweekly injections to manage her MS, she barely made ends meet. Plus there were the medical bills from that first, awful attack, before she'd even known why the vision out of her left eye sometimes went blurry or why her fingers occasionally felt numb. Sometimes she left rehearsal with such crippling fatigue she felt as if she were walking through Jell-O. She'd blamed it on the stress of dealing with her grandmother's recent illness. She'd blamed it on the rigorous physical demands of her solo role in the company production of *Giselle*. Mostly, though, she'd simply ignored her symptoms because she couldn't quite face the prospect that something was seriously wrong.

Then one night she'd fallen out of a pirouette. Onstage, midperformance. The fact that she'd been unable to peel herself off the floor had only made matters worse.

And now she'd never perform again.

Sometimes, in her most unguarded moments, Ophelia found herself pointing her toes and moving her foot in the familiar, sweeping motion of a rond de jambe. Then she'd close her eyes and remember the sickening thud as she'd come down on the wooden stage floor. She'd remember the pitying expressions on the faces of her fellow dancers and the way the crimson stage curtains had drawn closed on the spectacle with a solemn hush. Her career, her life, everything she'd worked for, had ended with that whisper of red velvet.

She had every reason to be grateful, though. She had a nice apartment in Manhattan. She had clothes on her back and a job. She'd even had the forethought to enroll in school while she'd been dancing, because she'd known that the day would come when she'd be unable to dance for a living. She just hadn't realized that day would come so soon. She'd thought she'd had time. So much time. Time to dance, time to love, time to dream.

She'd never planned on spending her Friday nights feeding kittens at an animal shelter, but it wasn't such a bad place to be. She actually enjoyed it quite a bit.

"I'll be careful, Beth. I promise." Ophelia draped a towel over the front of her dress and reached into the cabinet above a row of cat enclosures for a bottle and a fresh can of kitten formula.

As she cracked the can open and positioned it over the tiny bottle, her gaze flitted to the cage in the corner. Her hand paused midpour when she realized the wire pen was empty.

"Where's the little white kitten?" she asked, fighting against the rapidly forming lump in her throat.

"She hasn't been adopted, if that's what you're wondering." Beth cast her a knowing glance. "She's getting her picture taken for some charity thing."

"Oh." Ophelia hated herself for the swell of relief that washed over her. The shelter's mission was to find homes for all their animals, after all. Everyone deserved a home. And love. And affection.

The lump in her throat grew tenfold. "That's too bad."

"Is it?" Beth lifted a sardonic brow.

Ophelia busied herself with securing the top on the bottle and lifting one of the squirming kittens out of the pen lined with a heating pad that served as a makeshift incubator. "Of course it is."

She steadfastly refused to meet Beth's gaze, lest she give away her true feelings on the matter, inappropriate as they were.

But there was no fooling Beth. "For the life of me, I don't know why you won't just adopt her. Don't get me wrong—I appreciate your help around here. But I have a sneaky suspicion that the reason you came by tonight has more to do with visiting your fluffy friend than with feeding our hungry little monsters. You're besotted with that cat."

"And you're exaggerating." The orange kitten in Ophelia's hand mewed at a volume that belied its tiny size. Ophelia nestled the poor thing against her chest, and it began suckling on the bottle at once. "Besides, I told you. I can't have a pet. My apartment doesn't allow them."

It was a shameless lie. But how else was she supposed to explain her reluctance to adopt an animal she so clearly adored?

The truth was that she'd love to adopt the white Persian mix. She'd love coming home to the sound of its dainty feet pattering across the floor of her empty apartment. If the cat could come live with her, Ophelia would let it sleep at the foot of her bed, and feed it gourmet food from a can. If...

But she couldn't do it. She was in no condition to let anyone depend on her for their survival. Not even an animal. She was a ticking time bomb with an unknown deadline for detonation.

Ophelia braced herself for an ardent sales pitch. Beth obviously wasn't buying the excuses she'd manufactured. Fortunately, before Beth went into full-on lecture mode, they were interrupted by none other than the adorable white cat they'd been discussing. The snow-white feline entered the room in the arms of a statuesque woman dressed in a glittering, sequined floor-length dress.

Ophelia was so momentarily confused to see a woman wearing an evening gown at the animal shelter that at first she didn't seem to notice that the sequin-clad Barbie was also on the arm of a companion. And that companion was none other than Artem Drake.

Him.

Again? Seriously?

She could hardly believe her eyes. What on earth was he doing here?

For some ridiculous reason, Ophelia's first instinct was to hide. She didn't want to see him again. Especially here. Now. When he had a glamorous supermodel draped all over him and Ophelia was sitting in a plastic chair, chest covered in stained terry cloth while she bottle-fed a yelping orange tabby. And, oh, God, he was dressed in another perfect tuxedo. Had the man come strutting out of the womb in black tie?

She wondered what he'd look like in something more casual, a pair of soft faded jeans, maybe. Shirtless. Heck, as long as she was fantasizing, bottomless. Then she wondered why, exactly, she was wondering about such things.

"My, my, who do we have here?" Artem tilted his head.

Ophelia had been so busy dreaming of what he had going on beneath all that sleek Armani wool that she'd neglected to make herself invisible. Super.

"Um…" She struggled for something to say as his gaze dropped to her chest. Her nipples went tingly under his inspection, until she realized he was looking at the kitten, not her. Of course.

Why, oh, why hadn't she gone straight home after work?

He lifted his gaze so that he was once again looking her directly in the eyes. "Miss Rose, we meet again."

"You two know each other?" Beth asked, head swiveling back and forth between Ophelia and Artem.

Ophelia shook her head and centered all her concentration on not being attracted to him, while the orange kitten squirmed against her chest. "No, not really," she said.

"Why, yes. Yes, we do," Artem said at that exact instant.

The grin on his face was nothing short of suggestive. Or maybe that was just his default expression. Resting playboy face.

Heat pooled in her center, much to her mortification and surprise. She couldn't remember the last time she'd experienced anything remotely resembling desire. Unless this morning in the kitchen of Drake Diamonds counted. Which, if she was being honest, it most definitely did.

Beth frowned. Artem's date lifted an agitated brow.

Ophelia clarified the matter before Ms. Supermodel got the wrong idea and thought she was one of his sexual conquests, which no doubt were plentiful. "We've met. But we don't actually know one another." *Not at all*.

Artem directed his attention toward Beth and, by way of explanation, said, "Miss Rose works for me."

Worked, past tense, since he'd resigned from his family's business. Who did that, anyway?

"Drake Diamonds." Beth nodded. "Of course. Ophelia's told me all about it. I'm sure I don't need to tell you what a treasure you've found in her. She's one of our best volunteers. Such a hard worker."

"A hard worker," Artem echoed, with only a subtle hint of sarcasm in his smoky voice. Then, presumably to ensure that Ophelia knew he hadn't forgotten about her indiscretion in the kitchen, he flashed a wink in her direction. "Quite."

The wink floated through her in a riot of awareness. *He's not flirting with you. He's goading you.* There was a difference. Right?

Beth continued gushing, oblivious to Artem's sarcastic undertones. "I don't know what we'd do without her. She's such a cat lover, here almost every night of the week. Weekends, too."

So now she sounded like a lonely cat lady. Perfect. "Beth, I'm sure Mr. Drake isn't here to hear about my volunteer work." Again, why exactly *was* he here?

"Oh, sorry. Of course he isn't. Mr. Drake, thank you so much for the generous donation on behalf of your family, as well as for being photographed with one of our charges. Having your picture in the newspaper with one of the animals will definitely bring attention to our cause." Beth beamed at Artem.

So he'd given a donation to the shelter. A *generous* donation…and right when Ophelia had been wishing for something that would make him seem less appealing. Thank goodness she'd no longer be running into him at work. He was too…too *much*.

"My pleasure," Artem said smoothly, and ran a manly hand over the white kitty still nestled in his date's arms.

Ophelia's kitty.

Not hers, technically. Not hers at all. But that didn't stop the sting of possessiveness she felt as she watched the cat being cuddled by someone else. And not just *any*one else. Someone who was clearly on a date with Artem Drake.

It shouldn't have mattered, but it did. Very much.

"That's actually Ophelia's favorite cat you have there." Beth smiled.

"She's awfully sweet," Artem's date cooed.

Ophelia felt sick all of a sudden. What if Artem's companion adopted it? *Her* cat? She took a deep breath and fought against the image that sprang to her mind of the woman and Artem in the back of a stretch limo with the white kitten nestled between them. Did everything in life have to be so unfair?

"Is it now?" Artem slid his gaze toward Ophelia. "Your favorite?"

She nodded. There was no sense denying it, especially since she had that odd transparent feeling again. Like he could see straight into her heart.

"I keep insisting Ophelia should adopt her." An awkward smile creased Beth's face. Artem's date still had a firm grip on the kitten. Clearly, Beth was hinting that Ophelia needed to speak now or forever hold her peace.

She needed to get out of here before she did something monumentally stupid like snatch the kitten out of the woman's arms.

"I should be going." Ophelia stood and returned the tiny orange kitten to the incubator. "It was lovely seeing you again, Mr. Drake. Beth."

She nodded at Artem's date, whose name she still didn't know, and kept her gaze glued to the floor so she wouldn't have to see the kitten purring away in the woman's arms.

Artem ignored Ophelia's farewell altogether and looked right past her, toward Beth. "How much is the kitten? I'd like to purchase it for Miss Rose."

What?

"That would be delightful, Mr. Drake. The adoption fee is fifty dollars, but of course we'll waive it for one of our generous donors." Beth beamed.

Artem plucked the kitten out of his date's arms. Ophelia had to give the woman credit; she didn't hesitate to hand over the cat, but kept a firm grip on Artem's bicep. Ophelia felt like reassuring her. *He's all yours.* She wasn't going home with her former boss.

Nor was she going home with the kitten. "Mr. Drake, I need to have a word with you. *Alone.*"

Beth weaved her arm around Artem's date's elbow and peeled her away. "Come with me, dear. I'll give you a tour of our facility."

Beth gave Ophelia a parting wink as she ushered the woman out the door toward the large kennels. Surely she wasn't trying to play matchmaker. That would have been absurd. Then again, everything about this situation was absurd.

Ophelia crossed her arms and glared at Artem. "What do you think you're doing?"

He shrugged. "Buying you a cat. Consider it an early Christmas bonus. You're welcome, by the way."

"No." She shook her head.

Was he insane? And did he have to stand there, looking so unbelievably hot in that tuxedo, while he stroked the kitten like he was Mr. December in a billionaires-with-baby-animals wall calendar?

"No?" His blue eyes went steely. Clearly, he'd never heard such a sentiment come out of a woman's mouth before.

"No. Thank you. It's a generous gesture, but…" She glanced at the kitten. Big mistake. Her delicate little nose quivered. She looked impossibly helpless and tiny snuggled against Artem's impressive chest. How was Ophelia supposed to say no to that face? How was she supposed to say no to *him*? She cleared her throat. "…but no."

He looked distinctly displeased.

Let him be angry. Ophelia would never even see him again. *That's what you thought this morning, too.* She lifted her chin. "I really should be going. And you should get back to your date."

"My date?" He smiled one of those suggestive smiles again, and Ophelia's insides went instantly molten. Damn him. "Is that what this is about? You're not jealous, are you, Miss Rose?"

Yes. To her complete and utter mortification, she was. She'd been jealous since he'd waltzed through the door with another woman on his arm. What had gotten into her?

She rolled her eyes. "Hardly."

"I'm not quite sure I believe you."

Ophelia sighed. "Why are you doing this?"

"What exactly is it that I'm doing?"

"Being nice." She swallowed. She felt like crying all of a sudden, and she couldn't. If she did, she might not ever stop. "Trying to buy me a cat."

He shrugged. "The cat needs a home, and you like her. Why shouldn't you have her?"

There were so many reasons that even if Ophelia wanted to list them all, she wouldn't have known where to start. "I told you. I can't."

Artem angled his head. "Can't or won't?"

He'd thrown back at her her own words from their encounter at Drake Diamonds, which made Ophelia bite back a smile. The man was too charming for his own good. "Mr. Drake, as much as I'd love to, I cannot adopt that cat."

He took a step closer to her, so close that Ophelia suddenly had trouble taking a breath, much less forming a valid argument for not taking the kitten she so desperately wanted. Then he reached for her hand, took it in his and placed it on the supple curve of the cat's spine.

The kitty mewed in recognition, and Artem moved their linked hands through her silky soft fur in long, measured strokes. Ophelia had to bite her lip to keep from crying. Why was he doing this? Why did he care?

"She likes you," he said. And as if he could read her mind, he added, "Something tells me you two need each other. You come here nearly every day. You want this kitten. You need her, but you won't let yourself have her. Why not?"

Because what would happen if Ophelia had another attack?

No, not *if.* When. Her illness was officially called relapsing-remitting MS, characterized by episodic, clearly defined attacks, each one more neurologically devastating than the last. Ophelia never knew when the next one

Chapter Three

Artem arrived at Drake Diamonds the next morning before the store even opened, which had to be some kind of personal record. He couldn't remember the last time he'd been there during off-hours. If he ever had.

Dalton, on the other hand, had been making a regular practice of it for most of his life. In recent years, for work. Naturally. But back when they'd been teenagers, when Dalton had been more human and less workaholic robot, Artem's brother had gotten caught with a girlfriend in the middle of the night, in the middle of the first-floor showroom, in flagrante delicto.

It remained Artem's favorite story about his brother, even if it marked the moment when he'd discovered that Dalton had been the only Drake heir who'd been

entrusted with a key to the family business while still in prep school.

He wished it hadn't mattered. But it had. In truth, it still did, even though those feelings had nothing to do with the business itself.

He'd never had any interest in hanging around the shop on Fifth Avenue. To the other Drakes, it was a shrine. To the world, it was a historic institution. Drake Diamonds had been part of the Manhattan landscape since its crowded, busy streets teemed with horse-drawn carriages. To young Artem, it had always simply been his father's workplace.

And now it was his. Same building, same office, same godforsaken desk.

What was he doing? Dalton didn't need him. Not really. Wasn't his brother in a better position to save the company? Dalton was the one familiar with the ins and outs of the business. His bedroom in Lenox Hill was probably wallpapered with balance sheets.

All Dalton's life, he'd worn his position as a Drake like a mantle, whereas to Artem it had begun to feel like a straitjacket. Now that his father was gone, there was no reason why he couldn't simply shrug it off and move on with his life. In addition to his recent promotion, he'd been left a sizable inheritance. Sizable enough that he could walk away from his PR position with the company and never again have his photo taken at another dull social event if he so chose. There was no reason in the world he should willingly get out of bed at an ungodly predawn hour so he could walk to the store and sit behind his father's desk.

Yet here he was, climbing out of the back of his black town car on the corner of Fifth Avenue and Fifty-seventh Street.

He told himself that his decision to stay on as CEO, at least temporarily, had nothing to do with Ophelia. Because that would be preposterous.

Yes, she was lovely. Beyond lovely, with her fathomless eyes, hair like spun gold and her willowy, fluid grace. And yes, he'd lost more sleep than he cared to admit thinking about what it would feel like to have those impossibly graceful legs wrapped around his waist as he buried himself inside her.

Her simplest gestures utterly beguiled him. Innocent movements, like the turn of her wrist, made him want to do wholly inappropriate things. He wanted to wrap his fingers around her wrists like a diamond cuff bracelet, pin her arms over her head and trace the exquisite length of her neck with his tongue. He wanted that more than he'd wanted anything in a long, long time.

Artem was no stranger to passion. He'd experienced desire before, but not like this. Nothing like this.

He found it frustrating. And quite baffling, particularly when he found himself doing things like sitting behind a desk, adopting animals and dismissing a perfectly good date, choosing instead to go home and get in bed before midnight. Alone.

His temples throbbed as he stepped out of the car and caught a glimpse of himself in the reflection of the storefront window. He'd dressed the part of CEO in a charcoal Tom Ford suit, paired with a smooth silk tie in that dreadful Drake Diamond blue. *Who are you?*

"Good morning, Mr. Drake." The store's doorman greeted him with a tip of his top hat and a polite smile.

Standing on the sidewalk in the swirling snow, clad in a Dickensian overcoat and Drake-blue scarf, the doorman almost looked like a throwback to the Victorian era. Probably because the uniforms had changed very little since the store first opened its doors. Tradition ruled at Drake Diamonds, even down to how the doormen dressed.

"Good morning." Artem nodded and strode through the door.

He made his way toward the elevator on the opposite side of the darkened showroom, his footsteps echoing on the gleaming tile floor. Then his gaze snagged on the glass showcase illuminated by a radiant spotlight to his right—home to the revered Drake Diamond.

He paused. Against its black velvet backdrop, the diamond almost appeared to be floating. The most brilliant star, shining in the darkest of nights.

He walked slowly up to the showcase, inspecting the glittering yellow stone mounted at the center of a garland necklace of white diamonds. Upon its discovery in a South African mine in the late 1800s, it had been the third largest yellow diamond in the world. Artem's great-great-great-great-great-grandfather bought it on credit before it had even been properly cut. Then he'd had it shaped and set in Paris—in a tiara of all things—before bringing it to New York and putting it on display in his new Fifth Avenue jewelry store. People had come from all over the country to see the breathtaking diamond. That single stone had put old man Drake's little jewelry business on the map.

Would it really be so bad to let it go? Drake Diamonds was world famous now. Sure, tourists still flocked to the store and pressed their faces to the glass to get a glimpse of the legendary diamond. But would things really change if it were no longer here?

He glanced at the plaque beneath the display case. It gave the history of the diamond, its various settings and the handful of times it had actually been worn. The last sentence of the stone's biography proclaimed it the shining star in the Drake family crown.

Artem swallowed, then looked back up at the diamond.

Ophelia's face materialized before him. Waves of gilded hair, sparkling sapphire eyes and that lithe, swan-like neck…with the diamond positioned right at the place where her pulse throbbed with life.

He blinked, convinced he was seeing things. A mirage. A trick of the mind, like a cool pool of glistening water before a man who hasn't had a drink in years.

It was no mirage. It was her.

Standing right behind him, only inches away, with her exquisite face reflected back at him in the pristine pane of glass. And damned if that diamond didn't look as though it had been made just for her. Placed deep in the earth billions of years ago, waiting for someone to find it and slip it around her enchanting neck.

"Beautiful, isn't it?" Her blue eyes glittered beneath the radiant showroom lights, lighting designed to make gemstones shimmer and shine. Somehow she sparkled brighter than all of them.

Beautiful, indeed.

"Quite," Artem said.

She moved to stand beside him, and her reflection slipped languidly away from the necklace. "Sometimes I like to come here and look at it, especially at times like this, when the store is quiet. Before all the crowds descend. I think about what it must have been like to wear something like this, back in the days when it was actually worn. It seems almost a shame that it's become something of a museum piece, don't you think?"

"I do, actually." At the moment, it seemed criminal the diamond wasn't draped around her porcelain neck. He could see her wearing it. The necklace and nothing else. He could imagine that priceless jewel glittering between her beautiful breasts, an image as real as the snow falling outside.

He shoved his hands in his pockets before he used them to press her against the glass and take her right there against the display case until the gemstone inside fell off its pedestal and shattered into diamond dust. The very idea of it made him go instantly hard.

And that's when Artem knew.

Ophelia did, in fact, have something to do with his decision to stay on as head of Drake Diamonds. She may have had *every*thing to do with it.

He ground his teeth and glared at her. He didn't enjoy feeling out of control. About anything, but most especially about his libido. Artem was a better man than his father had been. He had to believe that.

Ophelia blinked up at him with those melancholy eyes that made his chest ache, seemingly oblivious to the self-control it required for Artem to have a simple conversation with her. "Is it true that it's only been worn by three women? Or is that just an urban myth?"

"Yes, it's true." He nodded. A Hollywood star, a ballerina back in the forties and Diana Kincaid Drake. Only three. That fact was so much a part of Drake mythology that Artem wouldn't have been able to forget it even if he'd tried.

"I see," she whispered, her eyes fixed dreamily on the diamond. She almost looked as though she were trying to see inside it, to the heart of the stone. Its history.

Then she blinked, turned her back on the necklace and focused fully on Artem, her trance broken. "About our meeting..."

"Ah, yes. Our meeting." Out of the corner of his eye, he spotted Dalton making his entrance through the store's revolving door. Artem lowered his voice, although he wasn't quite sure why. He had nothing to hide. "Shall I assume my kitten is tucked snug inside your home, Miss Rose?"

"Yes." Her cheeks went pink, and her bow lips curved into a reluctant smile.

So he'd been right. She'd wanted that kitten all along. Needed it, even though she'd acted as though he'd been forcing it on her.

He'd done the right thing. For once in his life.

"So." She cleared her throat. "Shall I make an appointment with your assistant so I can show you my designs?"

"What did you name her?" he asked.

Ophelia blinked. "I'm sorry?"

"The kitten." Somewhere in the periphery, Artem saw the curious expression on his brother's face and ignored it altogether. "Have you given her a name yet?"

"Oh." Her flush deepened a shade, as pink as primroses. "I named her Jewel."

For some reason, this information took the edge off Artem's frustration. Which made no sense whatsoever. "Then I suppose you and I have business to discuss, Miss Rose. I'll have my assistant get you the details." He gave her a parting nod and headed to the elevator, where Dalton stood waiting. Watching.

Somehow it felt as if their father was watching, too.

Ophelia stood poised on the black-and-white marble terrace while snowflakes whipped in the frosty wind. Despite the chill in the air, she hesitated.

"Welcome to the Plaza, miss." A doorman dressed in a regal uniform, complete with gold epaulettes on his shoulders, bowed slightly and pulled the door open for her with gloved hands.

A hotel. Artem Drake had summoned her to a *hotel*. Granted, the Plaza was the most exclusive hotel in Manhattan, if not the world, but still.

A hotel.

Did he think she was going to sleep with him? Surely not. She was worried over nothing. He was probably waiting for her in the tearoom or something. Although, as refined as he might be, Ophelia couldn't quite picture him taking afternoon tea.

"Thank you." She nodded politely at the doorman. After all, this wholly awkward scenario wasn't his fault. She wondered if she was supposed to tip him for opening the door for her. She had no clue.

Crossing the threshold into the grand lobby of the Plaza was like entering another world. Another decade. She felt like she'd walked into an F. Scott Fitzgerald novel. The decor was opulent, gilded with an art deco flavor reminiscent of Jay Gatsby.

Ophelia found it breathtakingly beautiful. If she'd known such a place existed less than a mile from her workplace, she would have been coming here every afternoon with her sketchbook and jotting down ideas. Drawings of geometric pieces with zigzag rows of gemstones that mirrored the glittering Baccarat chandeliers and the gold inlaid design on the gleaming tile floor.

Maybe she'd do those designs. If this meeting went as well as she hoped, maybe she'd end up with a job in the design department and she could come here and sketch to her heart's content. And maybe she'd actually see some of her designs come to fruition instead of just taking up space in her portfolio.

She tightened her grip on her slim, leather portfolio. It was Louis Vuitton. Vintage. Another treasure she'd found in her grandmother's belongings. It had been filled to bursting with old photographs from Natalia Baronova's time at the Ballet Russe de Monte Carlo. Ophelia had spent days studying those photos when she'd come home from her time in the hospital.

In the empty hours when she once would have been at company rehearsal dancing until her toes bled, she'd relived her grandmother's legendary career instead. Those news clippings, and the faded photographs with her grandmother's penciled notations on the back, had kept Ophelia going. She'd lost her health, her family, her job. Her life. All she'd had left was school and her grandmother's memories.

Ophelia had clung to those memories, studied those images until she made them her own by incorporating what she saw into her jewelry designs. The result was an inspired collection that she knew would be a success...if only someone would give her a chance and look at them.

She took a deep breath. If there was any fairness at all in the world, this would be her moment. And that *someone* would be Artem Drake.

"May I help you, miss?" A man in a pristine white dinner jacket and tuxedo pants smiled at her from behind the concierge desk.

"Yes, actually. I'm meeting someone here. Artem Drake?" She glanced toward the dazzling atrium in the center of the lobby, where tables of patrons sipped glasses of champagne and cups of tea beneath the shade of elegant palm fronds. Artem was nowhere to be seen.

She fought the sinking feeling in her stomach. *It doesn't mean anything. He could simply be running late.*

"Mr. Drake is in penthouse number nine. This key will give you elevator access to the eighteenth floor." The concierge slid a discreet black card key across the desk.

Ophelia stared at it. She'd never been so bitterly disappointed. Finally, *finally*, she'd thought she'd actually spotted a light at the end of the very dark tunnel that had become her life. But no. There was no light. Just more darkness. And a man who thought she'd meet him at a hotel on her lunch hour just to get ahead.

The irony was that's exactly what everyone in the company had thought when she'd begun dating Jeremy, the director. The other dancers had rolled their eyes whenever she'd been cast in a lead role. As if she hadn't earned it. As if she hadn't been dancing every day until her toes bled through the pink satin of her pointe shoes.

It hadn't been like that, though. She'd cared for Jeremy. And he'd cared for her, too. Or so she'd thought.

"Miss?" The concierge furrowed his brow. "Is there something else you need?"

Yes, there is. Just a glimmer of hope, if you wouldn't mind...

"No." She shook her head woodenly, and reached for the card key. "Thank you for your help."

She marched toward the elevator, her kitten heels echoing off the gold-trimmed walls of the palatial lobby. She didn't know why she was so upset. Or even remotely surprised. She'd seen all those photos of Artem in the newspaper, out every night with a different woman on his arm. Of course he'd assumed she'd want to sleep with him. She was probably the only woman in Manhattan who *didn't*.

Except she sort of did.

If she was honest with herself—painfully honest—she had to admit that the thought of sex with Artem Drake wasn't exactly repulsive. On the contrary.

She would never go through with it, of course. Not now. *Especially* not now. Not *ever*. It was just difficult to think about Artem without thinking about sex, especially since she went weak in the knees whenever he looked at her with those penetrating eyes of his. Eyes that gave her the sense that he could see straight into her aching, yearning center. Eyes that stirred chaos inside her. *Bedroom eyes.* And now she was on her way to meet him. In an actual bedroom.

Bed or no bed, she would *not* be sleeping with him.

The elevator stopped on the uppermost floor. She squared her shoulders and stepped out, prepared to search for the door to penthouse number nine.

She didn't have to look very hard. It was the only door on the entire floor.

He'd rented a hotel room that encompassed the entire floor? She rolled her eyes and wondered if all his dates got such royal treatment. Then she reminded herself that this was a business meeting, not a date.

If she had any sense at all, she'd turn around and walk directly back to Drake Diamonds. But before she could talk herself into leaving, the door swung open and she was face-to-face with Mr. Bedroom Eyes himself.

"Mr. Drake." She smiled in a way that she hoped conveyed professionalism and not the fact that she'd somehow gone quite breathless.

"My apologies, Miss Rose. I'm on the phone." He opened the door wider and beckoned her inside. "Do come in."

Ophelia had never seen such a large hotel room. She could have fit three of her apartments inside it, and it was absolutely stunning, decorated in cool grays and blues, with sleek, modern furnishings. But the most spectacular feature was its view of Central Park. Horse drawn carriages lined the curb alongside the snow-covered landscape. In the distance, ice skaters moved in a graceful circle over the pond.

Ophelia walked right up to the closest window and looked down on the busy Manhattan streets below. Everything seemed so faraway. The yellow taxicabs looked like tiny toy cars, and she could barely make out the people bundled in dark coats darting along the crowded sidewalks with their scarves trailing behind them like ribbons. Snow danced against the glass in a dizzying waltz of white, drifting downward, blanketing the city below. The effect was rather like standing inside a snow globe. Absolutely breathtaking.

"Um-hmm. I see," muttered Artem, standing a few feet behind her with his cell phone pressed against his ear.

Ophelia turned and found him watching her.

He didn't so much talk *to* whoever was on the other end as much he talked *at* them. He sounded rather displeased, but even so, he never broke eye contact with her throughout the call. "Despite the fact that this seems a rather…questionable…time to make such a donation, we must honor our commitment. I know you don't like to involve yourself with the press, brother, but think about the headlines if we backed out. Not pretty. And might I add, it would be my face they'd print a photo of alongside the negative chatter. So that's my final decision."

The person on the receiving end of his tirade was clearly Dalton. Ophelia felt guilty about overhearing such a conversation, so she averted her gaze. No sooner had she looked away than she caught sight of an enormous bed looming behind Artem.

My God, it's a behemoth.

She'd never seen such a large bed. It could have fit a dozen people.

Her face went hot, and she looked away. But as Artem wrapped up his call, her gaze kept returning to the bed and its sumptuous, creamy-white linens.

"Again, my apologies." Artem tossed his phone on the nearby sectional sofa and walked toward her. "Please, let me take your coat. Do make yourself comfortable."

She took a step out of his reach. "Mr. Drake, I'm afraid you've got the wrong impression."

"Do I?" He stopped less than an arm's length away, just close enough to send a wave of awareness crashing over her, while at the same time not quite crossing the boundary of respectability. "And what impression is that?"

"This." She waved a shaky hand around the luxurious room, trying—and failing—to avoid looking at the bed.

Artem followed her gaze. When he turned back toward her, an angry knot throbbed in his jaw. He lifted an impetuous brow. "I'm afraid I don't know what you mean, Miss Rose. Do you care to elaborate?"

"This room. And that bed." Why, oh, why, had she actually mentioned the bed? "When I said I wanted to show you my designs, that was precisely what I meant. I've no idea why you arranged to rent this ridiculous suite. The hourly rate for this room must be higher than my yearly salary. It's absurd, and thoroughly inappropriate. I have no interest in sleeping with you. None. Zero."

She really wished she hadn't stammered on the last few words. She would have preferred to sound at least halfway believable.

Artem's eyes flashed. "Are you quite finished?"

"Yes." She ordered her feet to walk straight to the door and get out of there. Immediately. They willfully disobeyed.

"I live here, Miss Rose. This is my home. I did not, as you so boldly implied, procure a rent-by-the-hour room in which to ravage you on your lunch break." He paused, glaring at her for full effect.

He lived here? In a penthouse at the Plaza?

Of course he did.

Ophelia had never been so mortified in her life. She wanted to die.

Artem took another step closer. She could see the ring of black around the dreamy blue center of his irises, a hidden hint of darkness. "For starters, if my intention was to ravage you, I would have set aside far more than an hour in which to do so. Furthermore, I'm your employer. You are my employee. Despite whatever you may have heard about my father, sleeping with the staff is not the way I intend to do business. Occasionally, the apple does, in fact, fall farther from the tree than you might imagine."

Ophelia had no idea what he was talking about, but apparently she'd touched a nerve. For the first time since setting eyes on Artem Drake—her *boss*, as he took such pleasure in pointing out time and time again—he looked less than composed. He raked an angry hand through his hair, mussing it. He almost looked like he'd just gotten out of bed.

Stop. God, what was wrong with her? She should *not* be thinking about Artem in bed. Absolutely, definitely not. Yet somehow, that was the one and only thought in her head. Artem, dark and passionate, tossing her onto the mammoth-sized bed behind him. The weight of him pressing down on her as he kissed her, entered her...

Her throat grew tight. "Good, because I have no interest whatsoever in sleeping with my boss."

Been there, done that. Got the T-shirt. Never again.

Artem narrowed his gaze at her. "So you mentioned."

Ophelia nodded. She wasn't sure she could manage to say anything without her voice betraying her. Because the more she tried to convince him that she didn't want to sleep with him, the more she actually wanted to. Assuming it was possible to want two very contradictory things at the same time.

But apparently he did *not* want to sleep with her, which was fine. No, not merely fine. It was good. She should be relieved.

Then why did she feel so utterly bereft?

"Now that we've established how ardently opposed we both are to having sex with one another—" His gaze flitted ever so briefly to her breasts, or maybe she only imagined it, since her nipples felt sensitive to the point of pain every time he looked at her "—perhaps you should show me your designs."

Her designs. The very reason she'd come here in

the first place. She swallowed around the lump in her throat. "Yes, of course."

He motioned toward the sleek, dark table in the center of the room. Ophelia opened her portfolio and carefully arranged her sketches, aware of his eyes on her the entire time. She felt every glance down to her core.

He picked up the first of her four large pages of bristol paper. "What do we have here?"

She took a deep breath. *This is it. Try not to blow it any more than you already have.* "Those are a collection of rings. I call them ballerina diamonds."

The subtlest of smiles came to his lips. "Ballerina diamonds? Why is that?"

"Each ring has a large center stone. See? That stone represents the dancer. The baguettes surrounding the center diamond are designed to give the appearance of a ballerina's tutu." She gestured around her waist, as if she were wearing one of the stiff classical tutus that she once wore onstage.

"I see." He nodded.

She allowed herself to exhale while he studied her drawings. She hadn't realized how exposed she would feel watching him go over her designs. These pieces of jewelry were personal to her. Deeply personal. They allowed her to keep a connection to her old self, her former life, in the only way she could.

She wanted him to love them just as much as she did, especially since no one in the design department at Drake Diamonds would even agree to meet with her.

"These are lovely, Miss Rose," he said. "Quite lovely."

"Thank you."

"What do we have here? A tiara? It almost looks familiar." He picked up the final page, the one she was the most nervous for him to see.

"That's intentional. It's a modernized version of the tiara that once held the Drake Diamond."

He grew very still at the mention of the infamous jewel.

Ophelia continued, "As you know, the original tiara was worn by Natalia Baronova. My collection calls for the stone to be reset in a new tiara that would honor the original one. I think it would draw a great number of people to the store. Don't you?"

He returned the sketch to the stack of papers and nodded, but Ophelia couldn't help but notice that his smile had faded.

"Mr. Drake..."

"Call me Artem," he said. "After all, we did nearly sleep together."

He winked, and once again Ophelia wished the floor of his lavish penthouse would open up and swallow her whole.

She cleared her throat. "I want to apologize. You've been nothing but kind to me, and I jumped to conclusions. It's just that I was involved with someone at work once before, and it was a mistake. A big mistake. But I shouldn't have assumed..."

Stop talking.

She was making things worse. But she wanted to be given a chance so badly that she was willing to lay everything on the line.

"Ophelia," he said, and she loved the way her name

sounded rolling off his tongue. Like music. "Stop apologizing. Please."

She nodded, but she wasn't quite finished explaining. She wanted him to understand. She *needed* him to, although she wasn't sure why. "It's just that I don't do that."

He angled his head. "What, exactly?"

"Relationships." Heat crawled up her neck and settled in the vicinity of her cheeks. "Sex."

Artem lifted a brow. "Never?"

"Never," she said firmly. "I'm not a virgin, if that's what you're thinking. It's just not something I do." *Since my diagnosis...*

Maybe she should tell him. Maybe she should just spill the beans and let him know she was sick, and that's why she'd been so adamant about not adopting the kitten. It was why she would never allow herself to sleep with him. Or anyone else. Not that she'd really wanted to...until now. Today. In this room. With him.

She should tell him. Didn't she have an obligation to be honest with her employer? To tell the truth?

Except then he'd know. He'd know everything, and he wouldn't look at her anymore the way he was looking at her now. Not like she was something to be fixed. Not like she was someone who was broken. But like she was beautiful.

She needed a man to look at her like that again. Not just any man, she realized with a pang. *This* man. Artem.

He gazed at her for a long, silent moment, as if weighing her words. When he finally spoke, his tone was measured. Serious. "A woman needs to be adored, Ophelia. She needs to be cherished, worshipped." His gaze dropped to her mouth, and she forgot how to breathe. "Touched."

And, oh, God, he was right. She'd never in her life needed so badly to be touched. Her body arched toward him, like a hothouse orchid bending toward the light of the sun. She wrapped her arms around herself, in desperate need of some kind of barrier.

"Especially a woman like you," he whispered, his eyes going dark again.

She swallowed. "A woman like me?"

Sick? Lonely?

"Beautiful," he whispered, and reached to cup her cheek with his hand.

It was the most innocent of touches, but at that first brush of Artem Drake's skin against hers, Ophelia knew she was in trouble.

So very much trouble.

Chapter Four

It took Dalton less than a minute to confirm what Artem already knew.

"These designs are exceptional." Dalton bent over the round conference table in the corner of their father's office—now Artem's office—to get a closer look at Ophelia's sketches. "Whose work did you say this was?"

Artem shifted in his chair. "Ophelia Rose."

Even the simple act of saying her name awakened his senses. He was restless, uncomfortably aroused, while doing nothing but sitting across the table from his brother looking at Ophelia's sketches. He experienced this nonsensical reaction every time she crossed his mind. It was becoming a problem. A big one.

He'd tried to avoid this scenario. Or any scenario that would put the two of them in a room together again. He really had. After their electrically charged meeting in his suite at the Plaza ten days ago, he'd kept to himself as much as possible. He'd barely stuck his head out of his office, despite the fact that every minute he spent between those wood-paneled walls, it seemed as though his father's ghost was breathing down his neck. It was less than pleasant, to say the least. It had also been the precise reason he'd chosen to meet Ophelia in his suite to begin with.

He'd needed to get out. Away from the store, away from the portrait of his father that hung behind his desk.

Away from the prying eyes of his brother and the rest of the staff, most notably his secretary, who'd been his dad's assistant for more than a decade before Artem had "inherited" her.

Not that he'd done anything wrong. Ophelia was an employee. There was no reason whatsoever why he shouldn't meet with her behind closed doors. Doing so didn't mean there was anything between them other than a professional relationship. Pure business. He hadn't crossed any imaginary boundary line.

Yet.

He'd wanted to. God, how he'd wanted to. But he hadn't, and he wouldn't. Even if keeping that promise to himself meant that he was chained to his desk from now on. He needed to be able to look at himself in the mirror and know that he hadn't become the thing he most despised.

His dad.

Of course, there was the matter of the cat. Artem supposed animal adoption wasn't part of the ordinary course of business. But he could justify that to himself easily enough. Like he'd said, the kitten had been an early Christmas bonus. A little unconventional, perhaps, but not *entirely* inappropriate.

If he'd tried to deny that he wanted her, he'd have been struck down by a bolt of lightning. Wanting Ophelia didn't even begin to cover it. He craved her. He *needed* her. His interest in her went beyond the physical. Beneath her strong exterior, there was a sadness about her that he couldn't help but identify with. Her melancholy intrigued him, touched a part of him he seldom allowed himself to acknowledge.

Any and all doubt about how badly he needed to touch her had evaporated the moment she'd told him that she didn't allow herself the pleasure of sexual companionship. Why would she share something so intimate with him? Even more important, why couldn't he stop thinking about it?

Since their conversation, he'd thought of little else.

Something was holding her back. She'd been hurt somehow, and now she thought she was broken beyond repair. She wasn't. She was magic. Hope lived in her skin. She just didn't know it yet. But Artem did. He saw it in the porcelain promise of her graceful limbs. He'd felt it in the way she'd shivered at his touch.

If he'd indeed crossed a forbidden line, it had been the moment he'd reached out and cupped her face. Something electric had passed between them then. There'd been no denying it, which was undoubtedly why she'd promptly gathered her coat and fled.

Artem had made a mistake, but it could have been worse. Far worse. The list of things he'd wanted to do to her in that hotel room while the snow beat against the windows had been endless. He'd exercised more restraint than he'd known he'd possessed. The very idea of a woman like Ophelia remaining untouched was criminal.

Regardless, it wouldn't happen again. It couldn't. And since he could no longer trust himself to have a simple conversation with Ophelia without burying his hands in her wayward hair and kissing her pink peony mouth until she came apart in his hands, he would just avoid her altogether. It was the best way. The only way.

There was just one flaw with that plan. Ophelia's jewelry designs were good. Too good to ignore. Drake Diamonds needed her, possibly as much as Artem did.

"Ophelia Rose?" Dalton frowned. "Why does that name sound familiar?"

"Because she works here," Artem said. "In Engagements."

Dalton waved a hand at the sketches of what she'd called her ballerina diamonds. "She can do *this*, and we've got her working in sales?"

"*You* have her working in sales." After all, Artem hadn't had a thing to do with hiring her. "I'd like to move her to the design team, effective immediately. I've been going over the numbers. If we can fast-track the production of a new collection, we might be able to reverse some of the financial damage that Dad did when he bought the mine."

Some. Not all.

If only they had more time...

"Provided it's a success, of course," Dalton said. "It's a risk."

"That it is." But what choice did they have? He'd already investigated auctioning off the Drake Diamond. Even if he went through with it, they needed another course of action. A proactive one that would show the world Drake Diamonds wasn't in any kind of trouble, especially not the sort of trouble they were actually in.

Over the course of the past ten days, while Artem had been actively trying to forget Ophelia, he'd been doing his level best to come up with a way to overcome the mine disaster. It had been an effective distraction. Almost.

Time and again, he'd found himself coming back to Ophelia's designs, running his hands along those creamy-white pages of cold-press drawing paper. Obviously, given the attraction he felt toward Ophelia, promoting her was the last thing he should do. Right now, he could move about the store and still manage to keep a chaste distance between them. Working closely with her was hardly an ideal option.

Unfortunately, it happened to be the *only* option.

"Let's do it," Dalton said.

In the shadow of his father's portrait, Artem nodded his agreement.

Ten days had passed since Ophelia had shown Artem her jewelry designs. Ten excruciating days, during which she'd seen him coming and going, passing her in the hall, scarcely acknowledging her presence. He'd barely even deigned to look at her. On the rare occasion when he did, he'd seemed to see right through her. And morning after morning, he kept showing up on *Page Six*. A different day, a different woman on his arm. It was a never-ending cycle. The man went through women like water.

Which made it all the more frustrating that every time Ophelia closed her eyes, she heard his voice. And all those bewitching things he'd said to her.

A woman needs to be adored, Ophelia. She needs to be cherished, worshipped.

Touched.

Ophelia had even begun to wonder if maybe he was right. Maybe she did need those things. Maybe the ache she felt every time she found herself in the company of Artem Drake was real. It certainly felt real. Every electrifying spark of arousal had shimmered as real as a blazing blue diamond.

Then she'd remembered the look on Jeremy's face when she'd told him about her diagnosis—the small, sad shake of his head, the way he couldn't quite meet her gaze. There'd been no need for him to tell her their affair was over. He'd done so, anyway.

Ophelia had sat quietly on the opposite side of his desk, barely hearing him murmur things like, *too much*, *burden* and *not ready for this*. The gravity of his words hadn't even registered until later, when she'd left his office.

Because for the duration of Jeremy's breakup speech, all Ophelia's concentration had been focused on not looking at the framed poster on the wall behind him— the company's promotional poster for the *Giselle* production, featuring Ophelia herself standing en pointe, draped in ethereal white tulle, clutching a lily. She wasn't sure if it was poetic or cruel that her final role had been the ghost of a woman who'd died of a broken heart.

That was exactly how she'd felt for the past six months. Like a ghost of a woman. Invisible. Untouchable.

But when Artem had said those things to her, when he'd reached out and cupped her face, everything had changed. His touch had somehow summoned her from the grave.

She'd embodied Giselle's resurrected spirit dancing in the pale light of the moon, without so much as slipping her foot into a ballet shoe. Her body felt more alive than it ever had before. Liquid warmth pooled in her center. Delicious heat danced through every nerve ending in her body, from the top of her head to the tips of her pointed toes. She'd been inflamed. Utterly enchanted. If she'd dared open her mouth to respond, her heart would have leaped up her throat and fallen right at Artem's debonair feet.

So she'd done the only thing she could do. The smart thing, the right thing. She'd run.

She'd simply turned around and bolted right out the door of his posh Plaza penthouse. She hadn't even bothered to collect her designs, those intricate colored pencil sketches she'd labored over for months.

She needed to get them back. She *would* get them

back. Just as soon as she could bring herself to face Artem again. As soon as she could forget him. Clearly, he'd forgotten about her.

That's what you wanted. Remember?

"Miss Rose?"

Ophelia looked up from the glass case where she'd been carefully aligning rows of platinum engagement rings against a swath of Drake-blue satin. Artem's secretary, the one who'd given her the instructions to meet him at the Plaza a week and a half ago, stood on the other side, hands crossed primly in front of her.

Ophelia swallowed and absolutely forbade herself to fantasize that she was being summoned to the hotel again. "Yes?"

"Mr. Drake has requested a word with you."

A rebellious flutter skittered up Ophelia's thighs. She cleared her throat. "Now?"

The secretary nodded. "Yes, now. In his office."

Not the hotel, his office. Right. That was good. Proper.

It required superhuman effort to keep the smile on her face from fading. "I see."

"Follow me, please."

Ophelia followed Artem's secretary across the showroom floor, around the corner and down the hall toward the corporate offices. They passed the kitchen with its bevy of petits fours atop gleaming silver plates, and Ophelia couldn't help but feel a little wistful.

She took a deep breath and averted her gaze. At least all this was about to end, and she could go back to the way things were before he'd ever walked in on her scarf-

ing down cake. She assumed the reason for this forced
march into his office was to retrieve her portfolio.

Although wouldn't it have been easier to simply
have someone return it to her on his behalf? Then they
wouldn't have been forced to interact with one another
at all. He'd never cross Ophelia's mind again, except
when Jewel purred and rubbed up against her ankles. Or
when she saw him looking devastatingly hot in the society pages of the newspaper every morning. Or the other
million times a day she found herself thinking of him.

"Here you go." Artem's secretary pushed open the
door to his office and held it for her.

Ophelia stepped inside. For a moment she was so
awestruck by the full force of Artem's gaze directed
squarely at her for the first time since the Plaza that the
fact they weren't alone didn't even register.

"Miss Rose," he said. For a millisecond, his focus
drifted to her mouth, then darted back to her eyes.

Ophelia's limbs went languid. There was no legiti-
mate reason to feel even the slightest bit aroused, but
she did. Uncomfortably so.

She pressed her thighs together. "Mr. Drake."

He stood and waved a hand at the man sitting opposite him, whom Ophelia had finally noticed. "I'd like to
introduce you to my brother, Dalton Drake."

Dalton rose from his chair and shook her hand. Ophelia had never thought Dalton and Artem looked much
alike, but up close she could see a faint family resem-
blance. They had the same straight nose, same chiseled features. But whereas Dalton's good looks seemed

wrapped in dark intensity, Artem's devil-may-care expression got under her skin. Every time.

It was maddening.

"It's a pleasure to meet you, Miss Rose," he said, in a voice oddly reminiscent of his brother's, minus the timbre of raw sexuality.

Ophelia nodded, unsure what to say.

What was going on? Why was Dalton here, and why were her sketches spread out on the conference table?

"Please, have a seat." Dalton gestured toward the chair between him and Artem.

Ophelia obediently sat down, flanked on either side by Drakes. She took a deep breath and steadfastly avoided looking at Artem.

"We've been discussing your work." Dalton waved a hand at her sketches. "You have a brilliant artistic eye. It's lovely work, Miss Rose. So it's our pleasure to welcome you to the Drake Diamonds design team."

Ophelia blinked, unable to comprehend what she was hearing.

Artem hadn't forgotten about her, after all. He'd shown her designs to Dalton, and now they were giving her a job. A real design job, one that she'd been preparing and studying for for two years. She would no longer be working in Engagements.

Something good was happening. Finally.

"Thank you. Thank you so much," she breathed, dropping her guard and fixing her gaze on Artem.

He smiled, ever so briefly, and Ophelia had to stop

herself from kissing him right on his perfect, provocative mouth.

Dalton drummed his fingers on the table, drawing her attention back to the sketches. "We'd like to introduce the new designs as the Drake Diamonds Dance collection, and we plan on doing so as soon as possible."

Ophelia nodded. It sounded too good to be true.

Dalton continued, "The ballerina rings will be the focus of the collection, as my brother and I both feel those are the strongest pieces. We'd like to use all four of your engagement designs, plus we'd like you to come up with a few ideas for companion pieces—cocktail rings and the like. For those, we'd like to use colored gemstones—emeralds or rubies—surrounded by baguettes in your tutu pattern."

This was perfect. Ophelia had once danced the Balanchine choreography for *Jewels*, a ballet divided into three parts, *Emeralds*, *Rubies* and *Diamonds*. She'd performed one of the corps roles in *Rubies*.

"Can you come up with some new sketches by tomorrow?" Artem slid his gaze in her direction, lifting a brow as her toes automatically began moving beneath the table in the prancing pattern from *Rubies'* dramatic finale.

Ophelia stilled her feet. She didn't think he'd noticed, but she felt hot under his gaze all the same. "Tomorrow?"

"Too soon?" Dalton asked.

"No." She shook her head and did her best to ignore the smirk on Artem's face, which probably meant he was sitting there imagining her typical evening plans of hanging out with kittens. "Tomorrow is fine. I do have one question, though."

"Yes, Miss Rose?" Artem leaned closer.

Too close. Ophelia's breath froze in her lungs for a moment. *Get yourself together. This is business.* "My inspiration for the collection was the tiara design. I'd hoped that would be the centerpiece, rather than the ballerina rings."

He shook his head. "We won't be going forward with the tiara redesign."

Dalton interrupted, "Not yet."

"Not ever." Artem pinned his brother with a glare. "The Drake Diamond isn't available for resetting, since soon it will no longer be part of the company's inventory."

Ophelia blinked. She couldn't possibly have heard that right.

"That hasn't been decided, Artem," Dalton said quietly, his gaze flitting to the portrait of the older man hanging over the desk.

Artem didn't bat an eye at the painting. "You know as well as I do that it's for the best, brother."

"Wait. Are you selling the Drake Diamond?" Ophelia asked. It just wasn't possible. That diamond had too much historical significance to be sold. It was a part of the company's history.

It was part of *her* history. Her grandmother had been one of only three women to ever wear the priceless stone.

"It's being considered," Artem said.

Dalton stared silently down at his hands.

"But you can't." Ophelia shook her head, vaguely aware of Artem's chiseled features settling into a stern expression of reprimand. She was overstepping and she knew it. But they couldn't sell the Drake Diamond. She had plans for that jewel, grand plans.

She shuffled through the sketches on the table until she found the page with her tiara drawing. "Look. If we reset the diamond, people will come from all over to see it. The store will be packed. It will be great for business."

Ophelia couldn't imagine that Drake Diamonds was hurting for sales. She herself had sold nearly one hundred thousand dollars in diamond engagement rings just the day before. But there had to be a reason why they were considering letting it go. Correction: Artem was considering selling the diamond. By all appearances, Dalton was less than thrilled about the idea.

Of course, none of this was any of her business at all. Still. She couldn't just stand by and let it happen. Of the hundreds of press clippings and photographs that had survived Natalia Baronova's legendary career, Ophelia's grandmother had framed only one of them—the picture that had appeared on the front page of the arts section of the *New York Times* the day after she'd debuted in *Swan Lake*. The night she'd worn the Drake Diamond.

She'd been only sixteen years old, far younger than any other ballerina who'd taken on the challenging dual role of Odette and Odile, the innocent White Swan and the Black Swan seductress. No one believed she could pull it off. The other ballerinas in the company had been furious, convinced that the company director had cast Natalia as nothing more than a public relations ploy. And he had. They knew it. She knew it. Everyone knew it.

Natalia had been ostracized by her peers on the most important night of her career. Even her pas de deux partner, Mikhail Dolin, barely spoke to her. Then on opening night, the company director had placed that diamond tiara, with its priceless yellow diamond, on Natalia's head. And a glimmer of hope had taken root deep in her grandmother's soul.

Natalia danced that night like she'd never danced before. During the curtain call, the audience rose to its feet, clapping wildly as Mikhail Dolin bent and kissed Natalia's hand. To Ophelia's grandmother, that kiss had been a benediction. One dance, one kiss, one diamond tiara had changed her life.

Ophelia still kept the photo on the mantel in her grandmother's apartment, where it had sat for as long as she could remember. Since she'd been a little girl practicing her wobbly plié, Ophelia had looked at that photograph of her grandmother wearing the glittering diamond crown and white-ribboned ballet shoes, with a handsome man kissing her hand. Her grandmother had told her the story of that night time and time again. The story, the diamond, the kiss…they'd made Ophelia believe. Just as they had Natalia.

If the Drakes sold that diamond, it would be like losing what little hope she had left.

"Is that agreeable to you, Miss Rose?" Dalton frowned. "Miss Rose?"

Ophelia blinked. What had she missed while she'd been lost in the past? "Yes. Yes, of course."

"Very well, then. It's a date." Dalton rose from his chair.

Wait. What? A date?

Her gaze instinctively flew to Artem. "Excuse me? A date?"

The set of his jaw visibly hardened. "Don't look so horrified, Ophelia. It's just a turn of phrase."

"I'm sorry." She shook her head. Maybe if she shook it hard enough, she could somehow undo whatever she'd unwittingly agreed to. "I think I missed something."

"We'll announce the new collection via a press release on Friday afternoon. You and Artem will attend the ballet together that evening and by Saturday morning, the Drake Diamond Dance collection will be all over newspapers nationwide." Dalton smiled, clearly pleased with himself. And why not? It was a perfect PR plan.

Perfectly horrid.

Ophelia couldn't go out with Artem, even if it was nothing but a marketing ploy. She definitely couldn't accompany him to the ballet, of all places. She hadn't seen a live ballet performance since she'd been one of the dancers floating across the stage.

She couldn't do it. It would be too much. Too overwhelming. Too heartbreaking. *No. Just no.* She'd simply tell them she wouldn't go. She was thankful for the opportunity, and she'd work as hard as she possibly could on the collection, but attending the ballet was impossible. It was nonnegotiable.

"That will be all, Miss Rose," Artem said, with an edge to his voice that sent a shiver up Ophelia's spine. "Until Friday."

Then he turned back to the papers on his desk. He'd finished with her. Again.

Chapter Five

Ophelia looked down at the ring clamp that held her favorite ballerina engagement design. Not a sketch. An actual ring that she'd designed and crafted herself.

It was really happening. She was a jewelry designer at Drake Diamonds, with her own office overlooking Fifth Avenue, her own drafting table and her own computer loaded with state-of-the-art 3-D jewelry design software. She hadn't used such fancy equipment since her school days, but after spending the morning getting reacquainted with the technology, it was all coming back to her. Which was a good thing, since she clearly wasn't going to get any help from the other members of the design team.

She recognized the dubious expressions on the faces of the other designers. They looked at her the same way the ballet company members had when Jeremy had chosen her as the lead in *Giselle*. Once again, everyone assumed her relationship with the boss was the reason she'd been promoted. Except this time, she had no connection with her boss whatsoever.

At least that's what she kept telling herself.

She did her best to forget about office politics. She had a job to do, after all.

In fact, she'd been so busy adapting to her new reality that she'd almost managed to forget that she was scheduled to attend the ballet with Artem on Friday night. *Almost.* The fact that she wasn't experiencing daily panic attacks in anticipation of stepping into the grand lobby of Lincoln Center was due to good old-fashioned denial. She could almost pretend their "date" wasn't actually going to happen, since Artem had gone back to keeping his distance.

She'd seen him a grand total of one time since their meeting with Dalton. Just once—late at night after the store had closed. Ophelia had stopped to look at the Drake Diamond before she'd headed home to feed Jewel. She hadn't planned on it, but as she'd crossed the darkened showroom, her gaze had been drawn toward the stone, locked away in its lonely glass case. Protected. Untouched.

She'd begun to cry, for some silly reason, as she'd gazed at the gem, then she'd looked up and spotted Artem watching from the shadows. She'd thought she had, anyway. Once she'd swept the tears from her eyes, she'd realized there had been no one else there. Just her. Alone.

Her day-to-day communication at the office was mostly with Dalton. On the occasions when Artem needed something from her, he sent his secretary, Mrs. Burns, in his stead. So when Mrs. Burns walked into Ophelia's office on Friday morning, she wasn't altogether surprised.

Until the secretary, hands clasped primly at her waist, stated the reason for her visit. "Mr. Drake would like to know what you're wearing."

The ring clamp in Ophelia's hand slipped out of her grasp and landed on the drafting table with a clatter. "Excuse me?"

Four days of nothing. No contact whatsoever, and now he was trying to figure out what she was wearing? Did he expect her to take a selfie and send it to him over the Drake Diamonds company email?

Mrs. Burns cleared her throat. "This evening, Miss Rose. He'd like to know what you're planning to wear to the ballet. I believe you're scheduled to accompany him tonight to Lincoln Center."

Oh. That.

"Yes. Yes, of course." Ophelia nodded and tried to look as though she hadn't just jumped to an altogether ridiculous assumption. *Again.*

Maybe the fact that she kept misinterpreting Artem's intentions said more about her than it did about him. It *did*, she realized, much to her mortification. It most definitely did. And what it said about her, specifically, was that she was hot for her boss. Her kitten-buying, penthouse-dwelling, tuxedo-wearing playboy of a boss. *Ugh.*

She supposed she shouldn't have been surprised. After all, every woman on the island of Manhattan—and undoubtedly a good number of the men—would have willingly leaped into Artem Drake's bed. There was a big difference between the infatuated masses and Ophelia, though. They could sleep with whomever they wanted.

Ophelia could not. Not with Artem. Not with anyone. The fact that doing so would likely put her fancy new job in jeopardy was only the tip of the iceberg.

"Miss Rose?" Mrs. Burns eyed her expectantly over the top of her glasses.

Ophelia sighed. "Honestly, why does he even care what I wear?"

"Mr. Drake didn't share his reasoning with me, but I assume his logic has something to do with the fact that you're a representative of Drake Diamonds now. All eyes will be on you this evening."

All eyes will be on you.

Oh, God. Ophelia hadn't even considered the fact that she'd be photographed on Artem's arm. At the ballet, of all places. What if someone recognized her? What if they printed her stage name in the newspaper?

Then everyone would know. *Artem* would know.

She swallowed. "Mrs. Burns, do you suppose it's really necessary for me to be there?"

The older woman looked at Ophelia like she'd just sprouted an extra head. "The appearance is part of the publicity plan for the new collection. The collection that you designed."

Right. Of course it was necessary for her to go. She should *want* to be there.

The frightening thing was that part of her did want to be there. She wanted to hear the whisper of pointe shoes on the stage floor again. She wanted to smell the red velvet curtain and feel the cool kiss of air-conditioning in the wings. She wanted to wear stage makeup—dramatic black eyeliner and bright crimson lips. One last time.

She just wasn't sure her heart could take it. Not to mention the fact that she'd be revisiting her past alongside Artem. She didn't want to feel vulnerable in front of him. Nothing good could come from that.

But she didn't exactly have a choice in the matter, did she?

She did, however, have the power to deny his ridiculous request. "Tell Mr. Drake he'll know what I'm wearing when he sees me tonight. Not to worry. I'm fully capable of dressing myself in an appropriate manner for the ballet."

Artem's secretary seemed to stifle a grin. "I'll certainly pass that message along."

Of course, an hour later, Mrs. Burns was back in Ophelia's office with a second request regarding her fashion plans for the evening. Again Ophelia offered no information. She was sure she'd find something appropriate in Natalia's old things, but she couldn't think about it right now. Because thinking about it would mean it was really happening.

Then after lunch, Mrs. Burns was back a third time, with instructions for Ophelia to arrive promptly at

Artem's suite at the Plaza at seven o'clock. Drake Diamonds would send a car to pick her up a half hour prior.

Ophelia wanted to ask why on earth it was necessary to convene at his penthouse beforehand. Honestly, couldn't they just meet at Lincoln Center? But all this back and forth with Mrs. Burns was starting to get ridiculous.

Maybe one day, in addition to her office, her drafting table and her computer, Ophelia would eventually have her own secretary. Then there would be no need to communicate with Artem at all. They could simply talk to one another through their assistants. No lingering glances. No aching need in the pit of her stomach every time he looked at her. No butterflies.

Better yet, no temptation.

Artem glanced at the vintage Drake Diamonds tank watch strapped round his wrist. It read 7:05. Ophelia was late.

Brilliant.

He'd been on edge for days, and her tardiness was doing nothing to help his mood.

For once in his life, he'd exercised a modicum of self-control. He'd done the right thing. He'd kept his distance from Ophelia Rose. Other than one evening when he'd spied her looking at the Drake Diamond after hours, he hadn't allowed himself to even glance in her direction.

And he'd never been so bloody miserable.

She'd seemed so pensive standing in the dark, staring at the diamond, her face awash in a kaleidoscope of cool blues and moody violets reflected off the stone's surface. What was it about that diamond? If the prospect didn't sound so ridiculous, Artem would have believed it had cast some sort of spell over her. She'd looked so beautiful, so sad, that he'd been unable to look away as the prisms of color moved over her porcelain skin.

And when amethyst teardrops had slid down her lovely face, he'd been overcome by a primal urge to right whatever wrong had caused her sorrow. Then she'd seen him, and her expression had closed like a book. Thinking about it as he paced the expanse of his suite, he could almost hear the ruffle of pages. Poetic verse hiding itself away. Sonnets forever unread.

And now?

Now she was late. It occurred to him she might not even show. Artem Drake, stood up by his evening companion. That would be a first. It was laughable, really.

He had never felt less like laughing.

As he poured himself a drink, a knock sounded on the door. Finally.

"You're late," he said, swinging the door open.

"Am I fired?" With a slow sweep of her eyelashes, Ophelia lifted her gaze to meet his, and Artem's breath caught in this throat.

She'd gathered her blond tresses into a ballerina bun—fitting, he supposed—exposing her graceful neck and delicate shoulders, wrapped in a white fur stole tied closed between her breasts with a pearly satin bow. Her dress was blush pink, the color of ballet slippers, and flowed into a wide tulle skirt that whispered and swished as she walked toward him.

Never in his life had he gazed upon a woman who looked so timelessly beautiful.

Seeing her—here, now, in her glorious flesh—took the edge off his irritation. He felt instantly calmer somehow. This was both a good thing and a very bad one.

He shot a glance at the security guard from Drake Diamonds standing quietly in the corner of the room, and thanked whatever twist of fate had provided a chaperone for this moment. His self-control had already worn quite thin. And as stunning as he found her dress, it would have looked even better as a puff of pink on the floor of his bedroom.

"Fired? No. I'll let it slide this time." He cleared his throat. "You look lovely, Miss Rose."

"Thank you, Mr. Drake." Her voice went breathy. As soft as the delicate tulle fabric of her dress.

She'd been in the room for less than a minute, and Artem was as hard as granite. It was going to be an undoubtedly long night.

"Come," he said, beckoning her to the long dining table by the window.

Since they were already behind schedule, he didn't waste time on pleasantries. And chaperone or no chaperone, he needed to get her out of this hotel room before he did something idiotic.

"Artem?" Ophelia's eyes grew wide as she took in the assortment of jewelry carefully arranged on black velvet atop the table. A Burmese ruby choker with eight crimson, cushion-cut stones and a shimmering band of baguettes and fancy-cut diamonds. A bow-shaped broach of rose-cut and old European-cut diamonds with carved rock crystal in millegrain and collet settings. A necklace of single-cut diamonds alternating with baroque-shaped emerald cabochon drops. And so on. Every square inch of the table glittered.

Ophelia shook her head. "I don't understand. I've never seen any of these pieces before."

"They're from the company vault," Artem explained. "Hence the security detail." He nodded toward the armed guard standing silently in the corner of the room.

Ophelia followed his gaze, took in the security officer and looked back up at Artem. "But you're the CEO."

"I am indeed." *CEO.* Artem was beginning to get accustomed to the title, which in itself was cause for alarm. This was supposed to be temporary. "Insurance regulations require an armed guard when assets in excess of one million dollars leave the premises. Think of him as a bodyguard for the diamonds."

The security guard gave a subtle nod of his head.

Ophelia raised a single, quizzical brow. "A million dollars?"

"Of course, if I'd known what you'd planned on wearing tonight, I could have selected just one appropriate item instead of transforming my suite into the equivalent of Elizabeth Taylor's jewelry box."

"Oh." She flushed a little.

Had she been any other woman, Artem would have suspected her coyness to be an act. A calculated, flirtatious maneuver. But Ophelia wasn't just any other woman.

He'd seen her at the office. At work, she was bright, confident and earnest. Far more talented than she realized. And always so serious. Serious, with that ever-present hint of melancholy.

But whenever they were alone together, her composure seemed to slip. And by God, was it a turn-on.

Artem liked knowing he affected her in such a way. He liked knowing he was the one who'd put the pretty pink glow in her cheeks. He liked seeing her blossom like a flower. A lush peony in full bloom.

Hell, he loved it all.

"Wait." Ophelia blinked. "These aren't for me."

"Yes, Ophelia, they are. For tonight, anyway. Just a little loan from the store." He shrugged one shoulder, as if he did this sort of thing every night, for every woman he stepped out with. Which he most definitely did not. "Choose whichever one you like. More than one if you prefer."

Ophelia's hand fluttered to her neck with the grace of a thousand butterflies. "Really?"

"You're representing Drake Diamonds," he said, by way of explanation.

"I suppose I am." She gave a little tilt of her head, then there it was—the smile he'd been waiting for. More dazzling than the treasure trove of jewels at her disposal. "I think a necklace would be lovely."

She pulled at the white satin bow of her little fur jacket. At last. Artem's fingers had been itching to do that since she'd crossed the threshold. He hadn't. Obviously. The diamonds he could explain. Undressing her in any fashion would have stepped over that boundary line that he was still determined not to cross.

He wondered if his father had been at all cognizant

of that line. Had he thought, even once, about the ramifications of his actions? Or had he taken what he wanted without regard to what would happen to his family, his business, his legacy?

Artem's jaw clenched. He didn't want to think about his father. Not now. He didn't want to think about how he himself represented everything that was wrong with the great Geoffrey Drake. Artem Drake was nothing but a living, breathing mistake of the highest order.

And his father was always there, wasn't he? A larger than life presence. A ghost haunting those he'd left behind.

Artem was tired of being haunted. It was exhausting. Tonight he wanted to live.

He gave Ophelia a quiet smile. "A necklace it is, then."

Ophelia had never felt so much like Cinderella. Not even two years ago when she'd danced the lead role in the company's production of the fairy tale.

As for jewels, from the outrageously opulent selection at Artem's penthouse, she'd chosen a necklace of diamond baguettes set in platinum that wrapped all the way around her neck in a single, glittering strand. It fit almost like a choker, except in front it split into three strands, each punctuated with large, brilliant cut diamonds. The overall effect was somehow dazzling, yet delicate.

It wasn't until Artem had fastened it around her neck that he'd told her the necklace had once belonged to Princess Grace of Monaco. Ophelia had been concentrating so hard on not reacting to the warm graze of his fingertips against her skin that she'd barely registered what he'd said. Now, as she sat beside him in the sleek black limousine en route to Lincoln Center, her hand kept fluttering to her throat.

She was wearing Princess Grace's necklace. How was that even possible?

She wished her grandmother were alive to see her right now. Ordinarily, she never let herself indulge in such wishes. Natalia Baronova's heart would break if she knew about the illness that had ended her granddaughter's dance career. But wouldn't she get a kick out of seeing Ophelia dressed in one of her grandmother's vintage gowns, wearing Grace Kelly's jewelry?

She smiled and her gaze slid toward Artem, who was watching her with great intensity.

"Allow me?" he asked, reaching for the bow on her faux fur stole.

Ophelia gave him a quiet nod as he tugged on the end of the satin ribbon. He loosened the bow and opened the stole a bit. Just enough to offer a glimpse of the spectacular diamonds around her neck.

"There," he said. "That's better."

Ophelia swallowed, unable to move, unable to even breathe while he touched her. She'd dropped her guard. Only for a moment. And now...

Now he was no more than a breath away, and she could see her reflection in the cool blue of his irises. He had eyes like a tempest, and there she was, right at the center of his storm. Looking beautiful and happy. Full of life and hope. So much like her old self—the girl

who'd danced through life, unfettered and unafraid—
that she forgot all the reasons why she shouldn't kiss
this man. This man who had such a way of reminding
her of who she used to be.

Her heart pounded hard in her chest, so hard she was
certain he could hear it. She parted her lips and murmured Artem's name as she reached to cup his chiseled jaw. His eyes locked with hers and a surge of heat
shot straight to her lower body. She licked her lips, and
there was no more denying it. She wanted him to kiss
her. She wanted Artem's kiss and more. So much more.

His fingertips slid from her stole to her neck, down
her throat to her collarbone. There was a reverence in
his touch, like a blessing. And those words that had
haunted her so came flooding back.

*A woman needs to be adored, Ophelia. She needs to
be cherished, worshipped.*

"Mr. Drake, sir, we've arrived." The limo's intercom
buzzed, and the driver's voice startled some sense back
into Ophelia.

What was she *doing*?

She was letting a silly diamond necklace confuse
her and make her think something had changed when,
in fact, *nothing* had. She was still sick. And she always
would be.

"I'm sorry." She removed her hand from Artem's
face and slid across the leather seat, out of his reach. "I
shouldn't have… I'm sorry."

"Ophelia," he said, with more patience in his tone
than she'd ever heard. "It's okay."

But it wasn't okay. *She* wasn't okay.

As if she needed a reminder, Lincoln Center loomed in her periphery. Inside that building, dancers with whom she'd trained less than a year ago were getting ready to perform, winding pink ribbons around their ankles in dressing rooms filled with bouquets of red roses. Jeremy, the man who'd once asked her to marry him, was inside that building, too. Only he was no longer watching her go through her last-minute series of pliés and port de bras. He was watching someone else do those things. He was kissing someone else's cheek in the final moments before the curtain went up. Another dancer. An able-bodied girl. One who wouldn't have to be carried off the stage when she fell down because she'd lost her balance. One who could do more than three pirouettes before her vision went blurry. One who wouldn't have to give herself injections twice a week and be careful not to miss her daily 8000 IU of vitamin D.

A girl who wasn't broken.

Not that she missed Jeremy. She didn't. She'd confused her feelings for him with her love of dance. If she'd ever had a proper lover, that lover was ballet. Ballet had fed her soul. And now? Now she was starving. Her body needed to move. As did her heart. Her soul.

Artem reached for her hand, but she shook her head and fixed her gaze out the car window, where a group of paparazzi were gathered with cameras poised at the ready.

She couldn't let him touch her again. If she did, there was no telling what she'd do. She was too raw, too tender, too hungry. And Artem Drake was too...

...too *much*.

She'd just have to pretend, wouldn't she? She'd have to act as though the way he looked at her and the things he said didn't make her want to slip out of her fancy dress and slide naked into his lap right there in the back of the Drake Diamonds limousine.

Artem looked at her. Long and hard, until her hands began to shake from the effort it took to keep pretending she was fine. The driver cleared his throat, and Artem finally directed his gaze past her, toward the photographers waiting on the other side of the glass.

"Showtime," he muttered.

Yeah. Ophelia swallowed around the lump in her throat. *Showtime*.

Chapter Six

Artem smiled for the cameras. He made polite small talk. He answered questions about the press release that Dalton had issued earlier in the day announcing the new Drake Diamonds Dance collection. He did everything he always did in his capacity as public relations front man for the company.

It was business as usual. With one very big exception—this time, Ophelia stood beside him.

He'd been attending events like this one for the better part of his adult life, and rarely had he done so alone. Having a pretty woman on his arm went with the territory. Logically, Ophelia's presence shouldn't have made a bit of difference. Logic, however, had little to do with the torturous ache he felt when he placed his hand on the small of her back or cupped her elbow as they walked up the broad steps to the entrance of Lincoln Center. Logic certainly wasn't behind the surge of arousal he'd felt when he'd placed the diamonds around her graceful neck. Logic hadn't swirled between them in the backseat of the car. That had been something else entirely. Some forbidden form of alchemy.

The fulfillment of what had nearly happened in the limousine tormented him. The kiss that wasn't even a kiss. The look in her eyes, though. That look had been as intimate as if she'd touched her lips to his. Perhaps even more so.

He could still feel the riotous beat of her pulse as he'd traced the curve of her elegant neck with his fingertips. Most of all, he could still see the glimmer in her sapphire eyes as she'd reached out to touch his face. Eyes filled with insatiable need. Sweet, forbidden hunger that rivaled the ravenous craving he'd been struggling against since the moment he'd caught her eating that silly cake.

God, what was wrong with him? He was a grown man. A man of experience. He shouldn't be feeling this wound up over a woman he barely knew, particularly one whom he had no business sleeping with.

On some level he loathed to acknowledge, he wondered if what he was experiencing was in any way similar to what his father had felt any of the myriad times he'd strayed. But Artem knew that wasn't the case. His father had been a selfish bastard, with little or no respect for his wedding vows. End of story. Artem wasn't even married, for God's sake. With good reason. He didn't have any intention of repeating the past.

Besides, this attraction he felt for Ophelia was different in every possible way. *She* was different.

Maybe it was her vulnerability that he found so intriguing. Or perhaps it was her unexpected ballsy streak. Either way, this strange pull they felt toward one another was without precedent. That much had become clear in the back of the limousine. With a single touch of her hand on his face, he'd known that she felt it, too. Whatever this was.

And now here they were, in the grand lobby of Lincoln Center, surrounded by people and cameras and blinding flashbulbs. Yet for all the distractions, Artem's senses were aware of one thing and one thing only— the whisper-thin fabric of her lovely dress beneath his hand as he guided her through the crowd. Just a fine layer of tulle between his flesh and hers.

It was enough to drive a man mad.

He somehow managed to answer a few more questions from lingering reporters before handing the usher their tickets and moving beyond the press of the crowd into the inner lobby.

"Welcome, Mr. Drake." The usher smiled, then nodded at Ophelia. "Good evening, miss."

"Thank you," she said, glancing at the ticket stubs as he passed them back to Artem.

Artem kept his hand planted on the small of her back as he led her to the lobby bar. It took every ounce of self-control he possessed not to keep that hand from sliding down, over the dainty, delectable curve of her behind, in plain view of everyone.

Get ahold of yourself.

His hand had no business on her bottom. Not here, nor anyplace else. Things were so much simpler when he could stick to the confines of his office.

Just as Artem realized he'd begun to think of the corner office as his rather than his father's, Ophelia turned to face him. Tulle billowed beneath his fingertips. He really needed to take his hands off her altogether. He would. Soon.

"I haven't even asked what we're seeing this evening. What's the repertoire?" She frowned slightly, as if trying to remember something. Like she had a catalog of ballets somewhere in her pretty head.

Artem hadn't the vaguest idea. Mrs. Burns had handed him an envelope containing the tickets as he'd walked out the door at five o'clock. He examined the ticket stubs and his jaw clenched involuntarily.

You've got to be kidding me.

"Artem?" Ophelia blinked up at him.

"Petite Mort," he said flatly.

"Petite Mort," she echoed, her cheeks going instantly pink. "Really?"

"Really." He held up the ticket stubs for inspection.

She stared at them. "Okay, then. That's certainly… interesting."

He lifted a brow.

"Petite mort means 'little death' in French," Ophelia said, with the seriousness of a reference librarian. She'd decided to tackle the awkwardness of the situation head-on, apparently. Much to Artem's chagrin, he found this attitude immensely sexy. "It's a euphemism for…"

"Orgasm." Artem was uncomfortably hard. In the champagne line at the ballet. Marvelous. "I'm aware."

What had he done to deserve this? Fate must be seriously pissed to have dealt him this kind of torturous hand. Of all the ballets…

Petite Mort.

He'd never seen this performance. In fact, he knew nothing about it. Perhaps it wasn't as provocative as it sounded.

It didn't matter. Not really. His thoughts had already barreled right where they didn't belong. Now there was no stopping them. Not when he could feel the tender warmth of Ophelia's body beneath the palm of his hand. Not when she was right there, close enough to touch. To kiss.

He looked at her, and his gaze lingered on the diamonds decorating the base of her throat. That's where he wanted to kiss her. Right there, where he could feel the beat of her pulse under his tongue. There. And elsewhere.

Everywhere.

His jaw clenched again. Harder this time. *Petite Mort.* How was he supposed to sit in the dark beside Ophelia all night and not think about touching her? Stroking her. Entering her. How could he help but envision what she looked like when she came? Or imagine the sounds she made. Cries in the dark.

How could he not dream of the myriad ways in which he might bring about *her* little death? Her *petite mort.*

"Sir?" Somewhere in the periphery of Artem's consciousness he was aware of a voice, followed by the clearing of a throat. "Mr. Drake?"

He blinked against the image in his head—Ophelia, beneath him, bare breasted in the moonlight, coming apart in his arms—and forced himself to focus on the bartender. They'd somehow already made it to the front of the line.

He forced a smile. "My apologies. My mind was elsewhere."

"Can I get you anything, sir?" The bartender slid a pair of cocktail napkins across the counter, which was strewn with items for sale. Ballet shoes, posters, programs.

Artem glanced at the *Petite Mort* program and the photograph on its cover, featuring a pair of dancers in flesh-colored bodysuits, their eyes closed and limbs entwined. His brows rose, and he glanced at Ophelia to gauge her reaction, but her gaze was focused elsewhere. She wore a dreamlike expression, as if she'd gone someplace faraway.

Artem could only wonder where.

Ophelia had to be seeing things.

The pointe shoes on display alongside the *Petite Mort* programs and collectible posters couldn't possibly be hers. Being back in the theater was messing with her head. She was suffering from some sort of nostalgia-induced delusion.

She forced herself to look away from them and focus instead on the bartender.

"I hope you enjoy the ballet this evening." He smiled at her.

He looked vaguely familiar. What if he recognized her?

She smiled in return and held her breath, hoping against hope he didn't know who she was.

"Mr. Drake?" The bartender didn't give her a second glance as he directed his attention toward Artem.

Good. He hadn't recognized her. She didn't want her past colliding with her present. It was better to make a clean break. Besides, if anyone from Drake Diamonds learned who she was, they'd also find out exactly why she'd stopped dancing. She couldn't take walking into the Fifth Avenue store and having everyone there look at her with pity.

*Every*one or a certain someone?

She pushed that unwelcome question right out of her head. She shouldn't be thinking that way about Artem. She shouldn't be caressing his face in the back of limousines, and she shouldn't be standing beside him at the ballet with his hand on the small of her back, wanting nothing more than to feel the warmth of that hand on her bare skin.

And the repertoire. *Petite Mort.*

My God.

She sneaked another glance at the pointe shoes, mainly to avoid meeting her date's penetrating gaze. And because they were there. Demanding her attention. One shoe tucked into the other like a neat satin package, wound with pink ribbon.

They could have been anyone's pointe shoes, and

most probably were. The company always sold shoes that had been worn by the ballerinas. Pointe shoes that had belonged to the principal dancers sometimes went for as much as two-fifty or three hundred dollars, which provided a nice fund-raising boost for the company.

She told herself they weren't hers. Why would her shoes be offered for sale when she was no longer performing, anyway?

Still. There was something so familiar about them. And she couldn't help noticing they were the only pair that didn't have an autograph scrawled across the toe.

Beside her, Artem placed their order. "Two glasses of Veuve Clicquot Rosé, please."

He removed his hand from her back to reach for his wallet, and she knew it had to be her imagination, but Ophelia felt strangely unmoored by the sudden loss of his touch.

He looked at her, and as always it felt as though he could see straight inside her. Could he tell how fractured she felt? How being here almost made it seem like she was becoming the old Ophelia? Ophelia Baronova. "Anything else, darling?"

Darling.

He shouldn't be calling her darling. It was almost as bad as princess, and she hated it. She hated it so much that she sort of loved it.

"The pointe shoes." With a shaky hand, she gestured toward the pastel ballet shoes. "Can I see them please?"

"Of course, miss." The bartender passed them to her while Artem watched.

If he found it odd that she wanted to hold them, he

didn't let it show. His expression was cool, impassive. As always, she had no idea what he was thinking.

And for once, Ophelia didn't care. Because the moment she touched those shoes, she knew. She *knew*. If flesh had a memory, remembrance lived in the brush of her fingertips against the soft pink satin, the familiar heaviness of the shoe's box—its stiff square toe—in the palm of her hand and the white powder that stull clung to the soles from the backstage rosin box.

Ophelia had worn these shoes.

The ones she now held were custom-made by a shoemaker at Freed of London, as all her shoes had been. A maker who knew Ophelia's feet more intimately than she knew them herself. She remembered peeling back the tissue paper from the box the shoes had come in. She'd sewn the ribbons on them with her own hands. She'd pirouetted, done arabesques in them. She'd danced in them. She'd dreamed in them. They were hers.

She glanced at Artem, who was now busy paying for the champagne, and then fixed her gaze once again on the shoes clutched to her chest. She wanted to see. She needed to be sure.

Maybe she was imagining things. Or maybe she just wanted so badly to believe, she was spinning stories out of satin. Heart pounding, she unspooled the ribbons from around the shoes. Her hands shook as she gently parted the pink material and peered inside. Penned in black ink on the insole, as secret as a diary entry, were the words she most wanted to see:

Giselle, June 1. Ophelia Baronova's final performance.

The pointe shoes in her hands were the last pair of ballet slippers she'd ever worn.

"What have you got there?" Artem leaned closer, and Ophelia was so full of joy at her fortuitous discovery that she forgot to move away.

"Something wonderful." Not until she beamed up at him did she notice the intimacy of the space between them. But even then she didn't take a backward step. She was too happy to worry about self-preservation.

For once, she wanted to live in the moment. Like she used to live.

"I'd ask you to elaborate, but I'm already convinced. Anything that puts such a dazzling smile on your face is priceless as far as I'm concerned." Without breaking eye contact, Artem slid two one-hundred-dollar bills out of his slim leather wallet and handed them to the man behind the counter. "We'll take the shoes, too."

Unlike the kitten incident, Ophelia didn't utter a word of protest. "Thank you, Artem. Thank you very much."

He pocketed his wallet, lifted a brow and glanced curiously at the pointe shoes, still pressed lovingly to Ophelia's heart. "No arguments about how you can't accept them? My, my. I'm intrigued."

"Would you like me to argue with you, Mr. Drake?"

"Never," he said. "And somehow, always."

She shrugged, feigning nonchalance, while her heart beat wildly in her chest. Part of her, the same part that still yearned to kiss him with utter abandon, wanted to tell him the truth. But how could she possibly explain that the satin clutched to her chest was every bit as priceless as the Drake Diamond itself? Maybe even more so.

The pointe shoes her grandmother had worn for her final performance lived in a glass case at the Hermitage in Saint Petersburg, alongside the shoes of other ballet greats like Anna Pavlova and Tamara Karsavina. Ballerinas went through hundreds of pointe shoes during the course of their career. Usually more than a hundred pairs in a single dance season. But none was ever as special as the last pair. The pair that marked the end.

Until this moment, Ophelia hadn't even known what had become of them. She remembered weeping as a nurse at the hospital removed them from her feet the night she'd fallen onstage. Then there'd been the MRIs, the blood tests, the spinal tap. And then the most devastating blow of all. The diagnosis. In all the heartbreak, her pointe shoes had been lost.

Like so much else.

Jeremy must have taken them. And now by some twist of fate, she'd found them again. Artem had bought them for her, and somehow it felt as though he'd given her back a missing part of her heart. Holding the shoes, she felt dangerously whole again.

The massive chandeliers hanging from the lobby ceiling flickered three times, indicating the start of the performance was imminent.

"Shall we?" Artem gestured toward the auditorium with one of the champagne flutes.

Ophelia took a deep breath, suddenly feeling as light and airy as one of the tiny bubbles floating to the top of the glass in his hand. "Lead the way."

They were seated on the first ring in private box seats, which shouldn't have come as a surprise, but somehow did. Ophelia had never come anywhere near such prestigious seating in the theater. When she'd been with the ballet, she always watched performances from the audience on her nights off. But like the other dancers, she'd sat in the fourth ring, at the very tip-top of the balcony. The nosebleed section. Those seats sold for twenty dollars each. She couldn't even fathom what the Drake Diamond seats must have cost. No doubt it was more money than all the dancers combined got paid in a year.

What exactly did tens of thousands of dollars get you on the first ring of the theater? For one, it got you privacy.

The box was closed in all sides, save for the glorious view of the stage. Ophelia sank into her chair with the ballet shoes still pressed to her heart, and her stomach fluttered as she looked around at the gold crown molding and thick crimson carpet. This was intimacy swathed in rich red velvet.

The lights went black as Artem handed her one of the glasses of champagne. His fingertips brushed hers, and she swallowed. Hard.

But as soon as the strains of Mozart's Piano Concerto no. 21 filled the air, Ophelia was swept away.

The music seemed filled with a delicate ache, and the dancers were exquisite. Gorgeous and bare, in their nude bodysuits. There was no hiding in a ballet like *Petite Mort*. There were no fluffy tutus or elaborate costumes. Just the beauty and grace of the human body.

Ophelia had never danced *Petite Mort*. She'd never thought she had what it took to dance such a provocative ballet. It was raw. Powerful. All-consuming. In the way perfect sex should be.

Not that Ophelia knew anything about perfect sex. Or ever would.

No wonder she'd never danced this ballet. How could she dance something called *Petite Mort* when she'd never had an orgasm? Things with Jeremy hadn't been like that. He'd been more interested in the height of her arabesque than the height of passion. She'd never been in touch with her own sensuality. She'd done too much dancing and not enough living. And now it was too late.

She watched the couple performing the pas de deux onstage turn in one another's embrace, legs and arms intertwined, and she'd never envied anyone more in her entire life. Somehow, some way…if she had the chance, she'd dance the hell out of that ballet now.

If only she could.

She felt different about her body than she had before. More appreciative. Maybe it was knowing that she'd never dance, never make love, that made her realize what gifts those things were. Or maybe it was the way the man sitting beside her made her feel…

Like a dancer.

Like a woman.

Like a lover.

Artem shifted in his chair, and his thigh pressed against hers. Just the simple brush of his tuxedo pants against her leg made her go liquid inside. She slid her gaze toward him in the dark and found him watching her rather than the dancers onstage. Had he been look-ing at her like that the entire time?

Her breath caught in her throat, and the ache between her legs grew almost too torturous to bear. What was happening to her? The feeling that she'd had in the limo was coming back—the desire, the need. Only this time, she didn't think she had the power to resist it. It was the shoes. They'd unearthed a boldness in her. Ophelia Baronova was struggling to break through, like cream rising to the top of a decadent dessert.

The shoes in her hands felt like a sign. A sign that she could have everything she wanted.

Just this once.

One last time.

Another dance. Another chance.

Intermission came too soon. Ophelia's head was still filled with Mozart and dark decadence when the lights went up. She turned to face Artem and found him watching her again.

"What do you think?" he whispered, and the atypi-cal hoarseness in his voice scraped her insides with shameless longing.

Just this once.

"I think when this is over—" she leaned closer, like a ballerina bending toward her partner "—I want to dance for you."

Chapter Seven

A better man would have stopped her.

A better man would have asked the limo driver to take her back to her apartment instead of sitting beside her in silent, provocative consent as the car sped through the snowy Manhattan streets toward the Plaza. A better man wouldn't have selected Mozart's Piano Concerto no. 21 once they'd reached the penthouse and she'd asked him to turn on some music.

But Artem wasn't a better man. And he couldn't have done things differently even if his overindulgent life had depended on it.

Instead he sat in the darkened suite watching as she slipped on the ballet shoes she'd chosen at Lincoln Center, and wound the long pink ribbons around her slender ankles. He could feel the music pulsing dead center in his chest. Or maybe that rhythmic ache was simply a physical embodiment of the anticipation that had taken hold of him since she'd leaned into him at intermission, eyes ablaze, face flushed with barely contained passion.

I want to dance for you.

Artem would hear those words in his darkest fantasies until the day he died.

"Are you ready, Mr. Drake?" Ophelia asked, settling in the center of the room with her heels together, toes pointing outward and willowy arms softly rounded.

So damned ready.

He nodded. "Proceed, Miss Rose."

The lights of Fifth Avenue drifted through the floor-to-ceiling windows, casting colorful shadows between them. When Ophelia began to move, gliding with slow, sweeping footsteps, she looked almost like she was waltzing through the rainbow facets of a brilliant cut gemstone. Outside the windows, snow swirled against the glass in a hushed assault. But a slow-burning simmer had settled in Artem's veins that the fiercest blizzard couldn't have cooled. His penthouse in the sky had never seemed so far removed from the real world. Here, now, it was only the two of them. He and Ophelia. Nothing else.

No other people. No ghosts. No rules.

I want to dance for you.

The moment Ophelia rose up on tiptoe, Artem knew that whatever was transpiring before him wasn't about ballet. This was more than dance. So much more. It was passion and heat and life. It was sex. Maybe even more than that.

The only thing Artem knew with absolute certainty was that sitting in the dark watching the adagio grace of Ophelia dancing for him was the single most erotic moment he'd ever experienced.

It was almost too much. The sultry swish of her ballerina dress, the exquisite bend of her back, the dizzying pink motion of her pointed feet—all of it. Artem had to fight against every impulse he possessed in order to stay put, to let her finish, when all he wanted was to rise out of his chair, crush his lips to hers and make love to her to the timeless strains of Mozart.

To keep himself from doing just that, he maintained a vise grip on the arms of the leather chair. Ophelia fluttered past him on tiptoe with her eyes closed and her lips softly parted, so close that the hem of her skirt brushed against his knee. Artem's erection swelled to the point of pain. Had he been standing, his arousal would have crippled him. Dragged him to his knees. For a moment, he even thought he saw stars. Then he realized the flash of light came from the diamonds around Ophelia's neck.

It didn't occur to Artem to wonder about the shoes or how she'd known they would fit. Nor did he ask himself how she could move this way. Questioning anything about this moment would have been like questioning a miracle. A gift.

Because that's what she'd given him.

Every turn of her wrist, every fluid arm movement, every step of her pink satin feet was a priceless gift. Then she stopped directly in front of him and began a dizzying sequence of elaborate turns, and he swore he could feel the force of each jackknife kick of her leg dead center in his heart. He could no longer breathe.

Artem wasn't sure how long Ophelia danced for him. Somehow it felt like both the longest moment of his life and, at the same time, the most fleeting. He only knew that when the music came to an end, she stood before him breathless and beautiful, with her breasts heaving and her porcelain skin glistening with exertion. And he knew that he'd never witnessed such beauty in his life. He doubted he ever would again.

Without breaking her gaze from his, Ophelia lowered herself into a deep curtsy. At last—at *long* last— Artem rose and closed the distance between them. As gently as he could manage while every cell in his body throbbed with desire, he took her hand in his and lifted her to her feet.

She rose up on the very tips of her toes, so that they were nearly eye level. When she smiled, it occurred to Artem that he'd never seen her so happy, so full of joy. Even her eyes danced.

He glanced down at her feet and the satiny pink ribbons that crisscrossed her ankles in a neat X.

"I used to be a dancer," she whispered, by way of explanation.

Used to be? *Used to be* was ridiculous. Artem didn't know what had happened in her past, but something clearly had. Something devastating. It didn't matter what that something was. He wasn't about to let it steal anything from her. Or make her believe she was anything else less than what she was.

"No." He took her chin in his hand. "Ophelia, you *are* a dancer."

Her eyes filled, and a single tear slipped down her lovely cheek. Artem wiped it away with the pad of this thumb.

He wished he had a bouquet of roses to place in her arms. Petals to scatter at her feet. She deserved that much. That much and more. But all he had to offer was the ovation rising in his soul. So he did what little he could. He brought her hand to his lips and pressed a tender kiss there.

"Artem." With a waver in her voice, she took a backward step, out of his reach.

For a single, agonizing moment, he thought she was going to run away again. To glide right out of the penthouse on her pink-slippered feet. He wouldn't let her. Not this time.

She didn't run, though. Nor did she say a word.

She simply reached her lithe arms behind her and unfastened the bodice of her strapless gown. Artem felt like he lived and died a thousand *petite morts* in the time it took her dress to fall away. It landed on his floor in a whispery puff of tulle, right where it belonged, as far as he was concerned.

She was gloriously naked, save for the diamonds around her neck, just as he'd imagined. Only no fantasy could have prepared him for the exquisite sight of her delicate curves, her rose-tipped breasts and all that marble-white flesh set off to perfection by the glittering jewels and the pink satin ribbons wrapped round her legs.

"Ophelia, my God." He swallowed. "You're beautiful."

* * *

Who is this woman I've become?

By putting on the shoes and dancing again, Ophelia had thought she could be her old self just for a moment. Just for a night. But this bold woman standing in front of Artem Drake and offering herself in every possible way wasn't Ophelia Baronova any more than she was Ophelia Rose. This was someone she didn't recognize. Someone she'd never had the courage to be.

Someone who actually believed Artem when he called her beautiful.

She *felt* beautiful, adorned in nothing but diamonds and pink satin shoes. Beautiful. And alive.

And aching.

She needed him to touch her. Really touch her. She needed it so much that she was on the verge of taking his hand and placing it exactly where she wanted it.

She stepped out of the pile of tulle on the floor and went to him, feeling his gaze hot on her exposed skin. Then she wrapped her arms around his neck, rose up en pointe and touched her lips ever so gently to his.

Artem let out a long, agonized groan, and to Ophelia, the sound was sweeter than Mozart. She'd never had such an effect on a man before. She'd never considered herself capable of it. And now that she knew she could—on this man, in particular—it was like a drug. She wanted to see him lose control, for once. She wanted him as raw and needy as she felt.

She got her wish.

His tongue parted her lips and he kissed her violently. Hard enough to bruise her mouth. He pulled her against him, and it seemed wholly impossible that this could be their first kiss. Their lips were made for this. For worshipping one another.

God, was it supposed to feel this way? So deliciously dirty?

She slid against him, reveling in the sensation of his wool tuxedo against her bare skin. Her eyes fluttered open as his mouth moved lower, biting and licking its way down her neck until he found her nipples. She cried out when he took her breast in his mouth, and a hot ribbon of need seemed to unspool from her nipple to between her legs. In the glossy surface of the snow-battered window, she caught a glimpse of their reflection and was stunned by what she saw—her bare body writhing against Artem, who had yet to shed a single article of clothing.

Before she could bring herself to feel an ounce of shame, he gathered her in his arms and carried her to his massive bed, that blanketed wonderland that had so intimidated her the first time she'd been here. Had it been only fourteen days ago that they'd sworn to one another they had no desire to sleep together?

She'd been lying then. Lying through her teeth. Ophelia had wanted this since the moment she'd set eyes on Artem Drake. No, not *this*. Not exactly. Because she hadn't known anything like *this* existed.

She struggled to catch her breath as Artem set her down on the impossibly soft sheets. Then he leaned over her and kissed her again, with long, slow thrusts of his tongue now, as if his body was telling her they had all the time in the world and he intended to make good use of every wanton second. As his hands found her hair and unwound her ballerina bun, she couldn't stop touching his face—his perfect cheekbones, his chiseled jaw and that secret place where his dimple flashed in those rare, unguarded moments when he smiled. The most beautiful man she'd ever seen, looking down at her as if he'd been waiting for this moment as long as she had. It hardly seemed possible.

He wound a finger in the diamonds around her neck and grinned as wickedly as the devil himself. "My grace."

Ophelia balled the sheets in her fists, for fear she might float away. Everything seemed to be happening so fast, yet somehow not quickly enough. She wasn't sure how long she could survive the heavenly warmth flowing through her. It was beginning to bear down on her. Hot and insistent. Then Artem moved his hand lower, and lower still, drawing a tremulous, invisible line down her body, until with a gentle touch he parted her and slipped his fingers inside her.

"Oh," she purred, in a voice she'd never heard come out of her mouth.

"Ophelia, open your eyes. Look at me."

She obeyed and found him watching her, his gaze filled with dark intention. His hand began moving faster. Harder, until she had to bite her lip to keep from crying out.

Before she knew what was happening, he'd begun kissing his way down her body. And were those really her breasts, arching obscenely toward his mouth?

And were those her thighs, pressed together, holding his hand in place?

Yes, yes they were. Artem's touch had made her a slave to sensation. She'd lost all ability to control her body, this body she'd once moved with such perfect precision.

Then his mouth was poised over her center, and she found she couldn't breathe for wanting.

"Please," she whimpered. *Oh, please.*

She wasn't even sure what she was begging for. Just some kind of relief from this exquisite torture.

"Shh," Artem murmured, and his breath fluttered over her, causing a fresh wave of heat to pool between her legs. It was excruciating. "I'm here, kitten."

Kitten.

Oh, God.

He pressed a tender kiss to the inside of one thigh, then the other, and the graze of his five o'clock shadow against her sensitive, secret places nearly sent her over the edge.

Then his mouth was on her, kissing, licking, tasting, and it was too much. She suddenly felt too exposed, too vulnerable. She was drowning in pleasure, and she knew that if she let it pull her under, there would be no turning back. No forgetting.

How could she return to normal life after this? How could she live the rest of her life alone, knowing what she was missing?

"Relax, kitten," Artem said in a hoarse whisper. He sounded every bit as wild and desperate as she felt. "I want to see you come. Let go."

He slipped a finger inside her again and she closed her eyes, tangled her fingers in his hair and held on for dear life. She didn't want to lose this moment to worry and fear. She wanted to stay. Here.

In this bed.

With this man.

So she did it. She let go. And the instant she stopped fighting it and let the blissful tide sweep her away, she shattered.

Stars exploded behind her eyes and she went completely and utterly liquid. She felt like she was blossoming from the very center of her being, and for the first time, the concept of *petite mort* made sense. *Little death.* Because it was like she'd died and gone someplace else. Somewhere dreamlike and enchanted. She could feel herself throbbing against Artem's hand, and it seemed as though he held her entire life force, every heartbeat she'd ever had, in the tips of his fingers.

And still he lapped and stroked, prolonging her pleasure, until it began to build again. Which seemed wholly unbelievable. She wouldn't survive it again. So soon? Was that even possible?

"Artem," she protested, even as she arched beneath him, seeking it again, that place of impossible light. Wanting him to take her there.

"Yes, kitten?" He pressed a butterfly-soft kiss to her belly and stood.

Ophelia had come completely apart, and there he was. Still fully dressed in a tuxedo, with his bow tie crooked just a fraction of an inch. He looked like he could have just walked out of a black-tie board of directors meeting…aside from the impressive erection straining the confines of his fly.

Ophelia swallowed. Hard. She needed to see him, to feel him.

Now.

She rose up on her knees and ran her hands over the expanse of his muscular chest. He cupped her breasts and pressed a kiss to her hair as she slid her palms under his lapels and pushed his jacket down his arms. It landed on the floor with a soft thud.

"Are you undressing me, Miss Rose?" he growled, and bent to take a nipple in his mouth. That crimson ribbon of need unwound inside her again, and she arched into him.

"I am." She sighed, dispensing with his shirt as quickly as she could manage. One of his cuff links flew off and bounced across the floor. Neither of them batted an eye.

She had no idea what she was doing. She'd never undressed a man in her life, but she was no longer nervous, hesitant or the slightest bit bashful. He'd unlocked something in her. Something no man had ever come close to discovering. Something wild and free.

She unzipped his fly and slid her hand inside, freeing him. He was hard—harder than she'd imagined he could possibly be—and big. Intimidatingly big. But the weight of his erection in her hands sent a thrill skittering up her spine.

She linked her gaze with Artem's and stroked him. He moaned, and his eyes went dark. Dreamy. *Bedroom eyes*, she thought. Watching him watch her as she pleasured him made her head spin. As if she'd done too many pirouettes. Ophelia's pulse pounded in the hollow of her throat, right where Princess Grace's diamonds nestled.

When she bent to take him in her mouth, Artem's hands found her hair. He wound her curls around his fingers and she could feel a shudder pass through him as surely as if it had passed through her own body. After this, after tonight, they would be tied to one another. Forever. Years from now, when her condition grew worse and she could no longer dance or even walk, she would remember this night. She would remember that she had once been cherished and adored. And when she closed her eyes and came back to this bed in her dreams, the face she would see in those stolen moments would be Artem's.

He might forget her someday. He probably would. There would be other women in his life, other mistresses. She wasn't foolish enough to believe that making love to her would change anything for him.

But it would change everything for her. It already had. *He* already had.

"Oh, kitten…" He hissed, and his fists tightened their grip on her hair.

She looked at up him. She wanted to etch this moment in memory. To somehow make it permanent.

He pulled her back up to her knees on the bed and rested his forehead against hers. "I need to be inside you," he whispered.

A knot lodged in her throat. Unable to speak, barely able to breathe, she nodded. *Yes, yes please.*

Then he was on top of her, covering her with the heat of his perfectly hard, perfectly male body. He stroked her face and kissed her closed eyelids as his arousal nudged at her center.

Ophelia had expected passion. She'd expected frenzy. And Artem had given her those things in spades. But this unexpected tenderness was more than she could bear. Then he groaned as he pushed inside, and she realized exactly how unprepared she'd been for the dangers of making love to Artem Drake.

Her pulse roared in her ears.

Remember.

Remember.

Remember.

Then with a mighty thrust, he pushed the rest of the way inside and Ophelia knew there would be no forgetting.

How could she ever forget the way the muscular planes of his beautiful body felt beneath her fingertips, or the glimmer of pleasured pain in his dark eyes, or the catch in her throat when at last he entered her? And the fullness, the exquisite fullness. She felt complete. Whole. Healed.

She knew it didn't make sense, and yet somehow it did. With Artem moving inside her, everything made sense. Because in that moment of sweet euphoria, nothing else mattered. Not her past, not her future, not even her disease. Nothing and no one else existed. Just she and Artem.

Which was the sort of thing someone in love would think.

But she wasn't in love with him. She couldn't be in love. With *anyone*. Least of all Artem Drake.

This was lust. This was desire. It wasn't love. It couldn't be. Could it?

No. Please no. No, no, no.

"Yes," Artem groaned, gazing down at her with an intensity that made her heart feel like it was ripping in half. Two pieces. Before and after.

"Yes," she whispered in return, and she felt herself nodding as she undulated beneath him, even as she told herself it wasn't true.

You don't love him. You can't.

She could feel Artem's heartbeat crashing against hers. She was free-falling again, lost in sensation and liquid pleasure. Her breath grew quicker and quicker still. She looked into his eyes, yearning, searching, and found they held the answers to all the questions she'd ever had. Somewhere behind him, snow whirled in dreamlike motion as he reached between their joined bodies to stroke her.

"Die with me, Ophelia," he whispered.

La petite mort.

Die with me.

With those final words, she perished once again and fell alongside Artem Drake into beautiful oblivion.

Chapter Eight

Artem slept like the dead.

Hours later, he woke to find Ophelia's shapely legs entwined with his and the pink ballet shoes still on her feet. Moonlight streamed through the windows, casting her porcelain skin in a luminescent glow. He felt as though he had a South Sea pearl resting in his arms.

What in the world had happened? He'd done the one thing he'd vowed he wouldn't do.

He wound a lock of Ophelia's hair around his fingers and watched the snow cast dancing shadows over her bare body. God, she was beautiful. Artem had seen a lot of beauty in his life—dazzling diamonds, precious gemstones from every corner of the earth. But nothing he'd ever experienced compared to holding Ophelia in his arms. She was infinitely more beautiful than the diamonds that still decorated her swan-like neck. Thinking about it made his chest ache in a way that would have probably worried him if he allowed himself to think about it too much.

There would be time for thinking later. Later, when he had to sit across a desk from her at Drake Diamonds and not reach for her. Later, when all eyes were on the two of them and he'd have to pretend he hadn't been inside her. Later, when he walked into his office and saw the portrait of his father.

He wasn't Geoffrey Drake. Artem may have crossed a line, but that didn't make him his father. He refused to let himself believe such a thing. Especially not now, with Ophelia's golden mane spilled over his pillow and her heart beating softly against his.

He let his gaze travel the length of her body, taking its fill. Arousal pulsed through him. Fast and hard. What had gotten into him? She'd reduced him to a randy teenager. Insatiable.

He should let her rest awhile. And should remove the pointe shoes from her feet so she could walk come morning.

He slipped out of bed, trying not to wake her, and gingerly took one of her feet in his hands. He untied the ribbon from around her ankle, and the pink satin slipped like water through his fingers. As gently as he could, he slid the shoe off her foot. She let out a soft sigh, but within seconds her beautiful breasts once again rose and fell with the gentle rhythm of sleep.

Artem cradled the pointe shoe in his hands for a moment, marveling at how something so lovely and delicate in appearance could support a woman standing on the tips of her toes. He closed his eyes and remembered Ophelia moving and turning across his living room. Poetry in motion.

He opened his eyes, set her shoe down on the bedside table and went to work removing the other one. It slipped off as quietly and easily as the first.

As he turned to place it beside its mate he caught a glimpse of something inside. Script that looked oddly like handwriting. He took a closer look, folding back the edges of pink satin to expose the shoe's inner arch.

Sure enough, someone had written something there.

Giselle, June 1. Ophelia Baronova's final performance.

Artem grew very still.

Ophelia Baronova?

Ophelia.

It couldn't be a coincidence. That he knew with the utmost certainty. It wasn't exactly a commonplace name. Besides, it explained why the shoes had fit. How she'd known she could dance in them. On some level, he'd known all along. Tonight hadn't been some strange balletic Cinderella episode. These were Ophelia's shoes. They always had been.

It explained so much, and at the same time, it raised more questions.

He studied the sublimely beautiful woman in his bed. Who was she? Who was she really?

He fixed his gaze once again on the words carefully inscribed in the shoe.

Baronova.

Why did that name ring a bell?

"I can explain." Artem looked up and found Ophelia holding the sheet over her breasts, watching him with a guarded expression. Her gaze dropped to the shoe that held her secrets. "It was my stage name. It's a family name, but my actual name is Ophelia Rose. I didn't falsify my employment application, if that's what you're thinking."

Her *employment application*? Did she think he was worried about what she'd written on a piece of paper at Drake Diamonds, while she was naked in his bed?

"I don't give a damn about your employment application, Ophelia." He hated how terrified she looked all of a sudden. Like he might fire her on the spot, which was absurd. He wasn't Dalton, for crying out loud.

"It's just—" she swallowed "—complicated."

Artem looked at her for a long moment, then positioned the shoe beside the other one on the nightstand and sat next to her on the bed. He could deal with complicated. He and complicated were lifelong friends.

He cradled her face in his hands and kissed her, slowly, reverently, until the sheets slipped away and she was bared to him.

This was how he wanted her. Exposed. Open.

He didn't need for her to tell him everything. It was enough to have this—this stolen moment, her radiant body, her passionate spirit. He didn't give a damn about her name. Of all people, Artem knew precisely how little a name really meant.

"Please," she whispered against his lips. "Don't tell anyone. Please."

"I won't," he breathed, cupping her breasts and lowering his head to take one of her nipples in a gentle, openmouthed kiss. She was so impossibly soft.

Tender and vulnerable.

As her breathing grew quicker, she wrapped her willowy legs around his waist and reached for him. "Please, Artem. I need you to…"

"I promise." He slid his hands over her back and pulled her close. Her thighs spread wider, and she began to stroke him. Slow and easy. Achingly so.

She felt delicate in his embrace. As small and fragile as a music-box dancer. But it was the desperation in her voice that was an arrow to his heart.

It nearly killed him.

Which was the only explanation for what came slipping out next. "I'm not really a Drake, Ophelia."

No sooner had the words left his mouth than he realized the gravity of what he'd done. He'd never confessed that truth to another living soul.

He should take it back. Now, before it was too late.

He didn't. Instead, he braced for her reaction, not quite realizing he was holding his breath, waiting for her to stop touching him, exploring him…until she didn't stop. She kept caressing him as her eyes implored him. "I don't understand."

"I'm a bastard," he said. "In the truest sense of the word."

"Don't." She kissed him, and there was acceptance in her kiss, in the intimate way she touched him. Acceptance that Artem hadn't even realized he needed. "Don't call yourself that."

His father had used that word often enough. Once he'd found out about Artem's existence, that is. "My real mother worked at Drake Diamonds. She was a cleaning woman. She died when I was five years old. Then I went to live in the Drake mansion."

Dalton had been eight years old, and his sister Diana had been six. Overnight, Artem had found himself in a family of strangers.

Wouldn't the tabloids have a field day with that information? It was the big, whopping family secret. And after keeping it hidden for his entire life, he'd just willingly disclosed it to a woman he'd known for a fortnight.

"Oh, Artem." Her lips brushed the corner of his mouth and her hands kept moving, kept stroking.

And there was comfort in the pleasure she offered. Comfort and release.

Artem didn't know her story. He didn't have to. Ophelia was no stranger to loss. Her pain lived in the sapphire depths of her eyes. He could see it. She understood. Maybe that was even part of what drew him toward her. Perhaps the imposter in her had recognized the imposter in him.

But he couldn't help being curious. Why the secrecy? *Slow down. Talk things through.*

But he didn't want to slow down. Couldn't.

"Kitten," he murmured, his breath growing ragged as he moved his hands up the supple arch of her spine.

She was so soft. So feminine. Like rose petals. And she felt so perfect in his arms that he didn't want to revisit the past anymore. It no longer felt real.

Ophelia was the present, and she was real. Nothing was as authentic as the way she danced. Reality was the swell of her breasts against his chest. It was her tender voice as she whispered in his ear. It was her warm, wet center.

Then there were no more words, no more confessions. She was guiding him into her, taking him fully inside. All of him. His body, his need, his truths.

His past. His present.

Everything he was and everything he'd ever been.

He didn't know what time it was when he finally heard the buzzing of his cell phone from inside the pocket of his tuxedo jacket, still in a heap on the floor. Pink opalescent light streamed through the windows, and he could hear police sirens and the rumble of taxicabs down below. The music of a Manhattan morning.

Artem wanted nothing more than to kiss his way down Ophelia's body and wake her in the manner she so deserved, but before he could move a muscle the phone buzzed again. Then again.

And yet again.

Artem sighed mightily, slid out of bed and reached for his tuxedo jacket. He fished his phone from the pocket and frowned when he caught his first glimpse of the screen. Twenty-nine missed calls.

Every last one of them was from his brother.

Bile rose to the back of his throat as he remembered the last time Dalton had blown up his phone like this. That had been two months ago, the night of their father's heart attack. By the time Artem had returned Dalton's calls, Geoffrey Drake had been dead for more than four hours.

He dialed his brother's number and strode naked across the suite, shutting himself in his small home office so he wouldn't wake Ophelia.

Dalton answered on the first ring. "Artem. Finally."

"What's wrong?" he asked, wondering why Dalton sounded as cheerful as he did. Artem wasn't sure he'd ever heard his brother this relaxed. Relaxing wasn't exactly the elder Drake's strong suit.

"Nothing is wrong. Nothing at all. In fact, everything is right." He paused. Long enough for alarm bells to start sounding in the back of Artem's consciousness. Something seemed off. "You, my brother, are a genius."

Now he was really suspicious. Dalton wasn't prone to flattery where Artem was concerned. Although he had to admit *genius* had a better ring to it than *bastard*. "What's going on, Dalton? Go ahead and tell me in plain English. I'm rather busy at the moment."

"Busy? At this hour? I doubt that." Artem could practically hear Dalton's eyes rolling. At least something was normal about this conversation. "I'm talking about the girl."

Artem's throat closed. He raked a hand through his hair and involuntarily glanced in the direction of the bed. "To whom are you referring?"

The girl.

Dalton was talking about Ophelia. Artem somehow just knew. He didn't know why, or how, but hearing Dalton refer to her so casually rubbed him the wrong way.

"Ophelia, of course. Your big discovery." Dalton let out a laugh. "She's not who we think she is, brother."

So the cat was out of the bag. How in the world had Dalton discovered her real name?

"I know." But even as he said it, he had the sickening feeling he didn't know anything. Anything at all.

"You know?" Dalton sounded only mildly surprised. "Oh. Well, that's good, I suppose. Although you could have told me about her connection to the Drake Diamond before I had to hear about it from a reporter at *Page Six*."

Artem froze.

The Drake Diamond? *Page Six?* What the hell was he talking about?

"I can't believe we've had Natalia Baronova's granddaughter working for us this entire time," Dalton said. "You did a good thing when you recommended her designs. A really good thing. Like I said, genius."

Baronova. No wonder the name had rung a bell. "You mean the ballerina who wore the Drake Diamond back in the forties? *That* Natalia Baronova?"

"Of course. Is there another famous ballerina named Natalia Baronova?" Dalton laughed again. He was starting to sound almost manic.

"Ophelia is Natalia Baronova's granddaughter," Artem said flatly, once he'd put the pieces together.

He remembered how passionately she'd spoken about the stone, the dreamy expression in her eyes when he'd spied her looking at it, and how ardently she'd tried to prevent him from selling it.

Why hadn't she told him?

I can explain.

But she hadn't explained, had she? She'd just said that Baronova had been a stage name. She'd said things were complicated. Worse, he'd let her get away with it. He'd actually thought her name didn't matter. Of course, that was before he'd known her family history was intertwined with *his* family business.

Artem had never hated Drake Diamonds so much in his life. He'd never much cared for it before and had certainly never wanted to be in charge of it. He could remember as if he'd heard them yesterday his father's words of welcome when he'd come to live in the Drake mansion.

I will take care of you. You're my responsibility and you will never want for anything, least of all money, but Drake Diamonds will never be yours. Just so we're clear, you're not really a Drake.

Artem had been five years old. He hadn't even known what the new man he called Father had even meant when he said, "Drake Diamonds." Oh, but he'd learned soon enough.

He should have tendered his resignation as CEO just like he'd planned. It had been a mistake. All of it. He'd stayed because of her. Because of Ophelia. He hadn't wanted to admit it then, but he could now. Now that he'd tasted her. Now that they'd made love.

It was bad enough that she had any connection to Drake Diamonds at all. But now to hear that she had a connection to the diamond… Worse yet, he had to hear it from his brother.

He should have pushed. He should have known

something was very wrong when she'd mentioned her employment application. He should have demanded to know exactly whom he'd taken to bed.

Instead he'd told her things she had no business knowing. Of course, she had no business in his bed, either. She was an employee. Just as his mother had been all those years ago.

Pain bloomed in Artem's temples. He'd been at the helm of Drake Diamonds for less than three months and already history had repeated itself. *Because* you *repeated it.*

"Natalia Baronova's granddaughter. I know. That's what I just said." Dalton cleared his throat. "I've set up a meeting for first thing Monday morning. You. Me. Ophelia. We've got a lot to discuss, starting with the plans for the Drake Diamond."

A meeting with Dalton and Ophelia? First thing Monday morning? Spectacular. "There's nothing to talk about. We're selling it. My mind is made up."

"Since when?" Dalton sounded decidedly less thrilled than he had five minutes ago.

"Since now." It was time to start thinking with his head. Past time. The company needed that money. It was a rock. Nothing more.

"Come on, Artem. Think things through. We could turn this story into a gold mine. We've got a collection designed by Natalia Baronova's granddaughter, the tragic ballerina who was forced to retire early. Those ballerina rings are going to fly out of our display cases."

Tragic ballerina? He glanced at the closed door that

led to the suite's open area, picturing Ophelia, naked and tangled in his sheets. Perfect and beautiful.

Then he thought about the sad stories behind her eyes and grew quiet.

"I'll crunch the numbers. It might not be necessary to sell the diamond," Dalton said. "Sleep on it."

Artem didn't need to sleep on it. What he needed was to get off the phone and back into the bedroom so he could get to the bottom of things.

Tragic ballerina...

He couldn't quite seem to shake those words from his consciousness. They overshadowed any regret he felt. "You mentioned *Page Six*. Tell me they're not doing a piece on this."

Not yet.

He needed time. Time to figure out what the hell was going on. Time to get behind the story and dictate the way it would be presented. Time to protect himself.

And yes, time to protect Ophelia, too. From what, he wasn't even sure. But given the heartache he'd seen in her eyes when she'd asked him to keep her stage name a secret, she wasn't prepared for that information to become public. Not now. Perhaps not ever.

Tragic ballerina...

He'd made her a promise. And even if her truth was infinitely more complicated than he'd imagined, he would keep that promise.

"Why on earth would you want me to tell you such a thing? The whole point of your appearance at the ballet last night was to create buzz around the new collection."

"Yes, I know. But..." Artem's voice trailed off.

But not like this.

"The story is set to run this morning. It's their featured piece. They called me last night and asked for a comment, which I gave them, since you were unreachable."

Because he'd been making love to Ophelia.

"You can thank me later. We couldn't buy this kind of publicity if we tried. It's a pity about her illness, though. Truly. I would never have guessed she was sick."

Artem's throat closed like a fist. He didn't hear another word that came out of his brother's mouth. Dalton might have said more. He probably did. Artem didn't know. And he didn't care. He'd heard the only thing that mattered.

Ophelia was sick.

Ophelia woke in a dreamy, luxurious haze, her body arching into a feline stretch on Artem's massive bed. Without thinking, she pointed her toes and slid her arms into a port de bras over the smooth surface of the bedsheets, as if she still did so every morning.

It had been months since she'd allowed her body to move like this. In the wake of her diagnosis, she'd known that she still could have attended ballet classes. Just because she could no longer dance professionally didn't mean she had to give it up entirely. She could still have taken a class every so often. Perhaps even taught children.

She'd known all this in her head. Her head, though,

wasn't the problem. The true obstacle was her battered and world-weary heart.

How could she have slid her feet into ballet shoes knowing she'd never perform again? Ballet had been her love. Her *whole* life. Not something that could be relegated to an hour or so here and there. She'd missed it, though. God, how she'd missed it. Like a severed limb. And now, only now—tangled in bedsheets and bittersweet afterglow—did she realize just how large the hole in her life had become in these past few months. But as much as she'd needed ballet, she'd need this more. *This.*

Him.

She'd needed to be touched. To be loved. She'd needed Artem.

And now…

Now it had to be over.

She squeezed her eyes closed, searching for sleep, wishing she could fall back into the velvet comfort of night. She wasn't ready. She wasn't ready for the harsh light of morning or the loss that would come with the rising sun. She wasn't ready for goodbye.

This couldn't happen again. It absolutely could not. No amount of wishing or hoping or imagining could have prepared her for the reality of Artem making love to her. Now she knew. And that knowledge was every bit as crippling as her physical ailments.

I'm not really a Drake, Ophelia.

Last night had been more than physical. So much more. She'd danced for him. She'd shown him a part of herself that was now hers and hers alone. A tender, aching secret. And in return, he'd revealed himself to her. The real Artem Drake. How many people knew that man?

Ophelia swallowed around the lump in her throat. Not very many, if anyone, really. She was certain. She'd seen the truth in the sadness of his gaze, felt it in the honesty of his touch. She hadn't expected such brutal honesty. She hadn't been prepared for it. She hadn't thought she would fall. But that's exactly what had happened, and the descent had been exquisite.

How could she bring herself to walk away when she'd already lost so much?

She blinked back the sting of tears and took a deep breath, noting the way her body felt. Sore, but in a good way. Like she'd exercised parts of herself she hadn't used in centuries. Her legs, her feet. Her heart.

It beat wildly, with the kind of breathless abandon she'd experienced only when she danced. And every cell in her body, every lost dream she carried inside, cried out, *Encore, encore!* She closed her eyes and could have sworn she felt rose petals falling against her bare shoulders.

One more day. One more night.

Just one.

With him.

She would allow herself that encore. Then when the weekend was over, everything would go back to normal. Because it had to.

She sat up, searching the suite for signs of Artem. His clothes were still pooled on the floor, as were hers. Somewhere in the distance, she heard the soothing cadence of his voice. Like music.

A melody of longing coursed through her, followed by a soft knock on the door.

"Artem," Ophelia called out, wrapping herself in the chinchilla blanket at the foot of the bed.

No answer.

"Mr. Drake," a voice called through the door. "Your breakfast, sir."

Breakfast. He must have gotten up to order room service. She slid out of bed and padded to the door, catching a glimpse of her reflection in a sleek, silver-framed mirror hanging in the entryway. She looked exactly as she felt—as though she'd been good and thoroughly ravished.

Her cheeks flared with heat as she opened the door to face the waiter, dressed impeccably in a white coat, black trousers and bow tie. If Ophelia hadn't already been conscious of the fact she was dressed in only a blanket—albeit a fur one—the sight of that bow tie would have done the trick. She'd never felt so undressed.

"Good morning." She bit her lip.

"Miss." Unfazed, the waiter greeted her with a polite nod and wheeled a cart ladened with silver-domed trays into the foyer of the suite. Clearly, he'd seen this sort of thing before.

Possibly even in this very room, although Ophelia couldn't bring herself to dwell on that. Just the idea of another woman in Artem's bed sent a hot spike of jealousy straight to her heart.

He doesn't belong to you.

He doesn't belong to you, and you don't belong to him. One more night. That's all.

She took a deep breath and pulled the chinchilla tighter around her frame as the waiter arranged everything in a perfect tableau on the dining room table. From the looks of things, Artem had ordered copious amounts of food, coffee and even mimosas. A vase of fragrant pink peonies stood in the center of the table and the morning newspapers were fanned neatly in front of them.

"Mr. Drake's standard breakfast." The young man waved at the dining area with a flourish. "May I get you anything else, miss?"

This was Artem's standard breakfast? What must it be like to live as a Drake?

Ophelia couldn't even begin to imagine. Nor did she want to. She would never survive that kind of pressure, not to mention the ongoing, continual scrutiny by the press...having your life on constant display for the entire world to see. Last night had been frightening enough, and she hadn't even been the center of attention. Not really. The press, the people...they'd been interested in the jewelry. And Artem, of course. She'd just been the woman on Artem Drake's arm. There'd been one reporter who had looked vaguely familiar, but she hadn't directed a single question at her. Ophelia had been unduly paranoid, just as she had with the bartender.

"Miss?" the waiter said. "Perhaps some hot tea?"

"No, thank you. This all looks..." Her gaze swept over the table and snagged on the cover of *Page Six*.

Was that a photo of *her*, splashed above the fold? She stared at it in confusion, trying to figure out why in the world they would crop Artem's image out of the picture. Only his arm was visible, reaching behind her waist to settle his hand on the small of her back. A wave of dread crashed over her as she searched the headline. And then everything became heart-sickeningly clear.

"Miss?" the waiter prompted again. "You were saying?"

Ophelia blinked. She was too upset to cry. Too upset to even think. "Um, oh, yes. Thank you. Everything looks wonderful."

She couldn't keep her voice from catching. She couldn't seem to think straight. She could barely even breathe.

The waiter excused himself, and Ophelia sank into one of the dining room chairs. A teardrop landed in a wet splat on her photograph. She hadn't even realized she'd begun to cry.

Everything looks wonderful.

She'd barely been able to get those words out. Nothing was wonderful. Nothing at all.

She closed her eyes and still she saw it. That awful headline. She probably always would. In an instant, the bold black typeface had been seared into her memory.

Fallen Ballet Star Ophelia Baronova Once Again Steps into the Spotlight...

Fallen ballet star. They made it sound like she'd died.

You did. You're no longer Ophelia Baronova. You're Ophelia Rose now, remember?

And now everyone would know. *Everyone.* Including Artem. Maybe he already did.

He'd promised to keep her identity a secret. Surely he

wasn't behind this. Bile rose up the back of her throat. She swallowed it down, along with the last vestiges of the careful, anonymous life she'd managed to build for herself after her diagnosis.

She felt faint. She needed to lie down. But most importantly, she needed to get out of here.

One more night.

Her chest tightened, as if the pretty pink ribbons on her ballet shoes had bound themselves around her heart. There wouldn't be another night.

Not now.

Not ever.

Chapter Nine

Beneath the conference table, Artem's hands clenched in his lap as he sat and watched Ophelia walk into the room on Monday morning. He felt like hitting something. The wall, maybe. How good would it feel to send his fist flying through a bit of Drake Diamonds drywall?

Damn good.

He couldn't remember the last time he'd been as angry as he had when he'd finally ended the call with Dalton and strode back to the bedroom, only to find his bed empty. No Ophelia. No more ballet shoes on his night table. Just a lonely, glittering strand of diamonds left behind on the pillow.

He'd been gone a matter of minutes, and she'd left. Without a word.

At first, he simply couldn't believe it. There wasn't another woman in all of Manhattan who would dare do such a thing. No other woman had even had the chance. Artem had firm rules about sleepovers. He didn't partake in them.

Until the other night.

Nothing about his involvement with Ophelia was ordinary, though, was it? Since the moment he'd first spotted her in the kitchen at Drake Diamonds, he'd found himself doing things he'd never before contemplated. Staying on as CEO. Adopting kittens. Exposing dark secrets. He scarcely recognized himself.

He sure hadn't recognized the man who'd stormed through the penthouse suite, angrily searching for something. A sign, perhaps? Some leftover trinket, a bit of pink ribbon that would ensure that he hadn't imagined the events of the night before. A reminder that it had all been real. That spellbinding dance. The intensity of their lovemaking…

Then he'd seen the newspaper lying on the dining table, and he'd known.

She'd been the cover story on *Page Six*, and the article had been less than discreet. Worse, Ophelia had clearly seen it before he'd had a chance to warn her. The newsprint had been wet with what he assumed were tears, the paper still damp as it trembled in his hands. He must have missed her getaway by a matter of seconds.

"Mr. Drake." Without quite meeting his gaze, Ophelia nodded as she entered the room.

So they were back to formalities, were they? It took

every ounce of his self-control not to remind her that the last time they'd seen one another, they'd both been naked. And gloriously sated.

Just imagining it made him go instantly hard, which did nothing to soothe his irritation.

"Miss Rose," he said, sounding colder than he'd intended. "Or should I call you Miss *Baronova*?"

She went instantly pale. "I prefer Miss Rose."

"Just checking." Artem did his best impression of a careless shrug.

He did care, actually. That was the problem. He cared far too much.

Multiple sclerosis.

My God, how had he not known she was sick? How had he looked into those haunted eyes as he'd buried himself inside her and not realized it?

Artem was ashamed to admit that although he'd donated money to the National MS Society and even attended a few of their galas, his knowledge of the condition was less than thorough. He'd spent a good portion of the weekend online familiarizing himself with its symptoms and prognosis.

The article in *Page Six* had offered little hope and predicted that Ophelia would eventually end up in a wheelchair. Artem found this conclusion wholly beyond his comprehension. The idea that she would never dance again was impossible for him to accept. And it made the gift she'd given him all the more precious.

The story alleged she hadn't danced at all since her diagnosis. Artem hadn't needed to read those words to know it was true. There'd been something undeniably sacred about the ballet she'd performed for him. He could still see her spinning and twirling on pink satin tiptoes. As he slept, as he dreamed...even while he was awake. It was all he saw. Day and night.

Dalton had stood as she entered the room. "Good morning, Ophelia," he said now.

"Good morning." She aimed a smile at his brother. A smile that on the surface seemed perfectly genuine, but Artem could see the slight tremble in her lips.

He knew those lips. He knew how they tasted, knew what it felt like to bite into their pillowy softness.

Ophelia's smile faded as she glanced at him, then quickly looked away. Being around him again clearly made her uncomfortable. Good. He'd felt distinctly uncomfortable every time he'd tried to call her since her disappearing act. He'd felt even more uncomfortable when his knocks on her apartment door had gone unanswered. He'd felt so *uncomfortable* he'd been tempted to tear the door off its hinges and demand she speak to him.

He could help her. Didn't she know that? He could hire the best doctors money could buy. He could fix her...if only she'd let him.

Dalton cleared his throat. "We have a few things to discuss this morning."

The understatement of the century perhaps. Although what could Artem actually say to Ophelia with Dalton present? Nothing. Not a damn thing.

Ophelia nodded wordlessly. As angry as he was, it killed him to see her this way. Quiet. Afraid. His arms itched to hold her, his body cried out for her, even if logically he knew it would never happen. She'd made that abundantly clear.

Artem should have been fine with that. He should have been relieved. He didn't want a *relationship*. Never had. He didn't want marriage or, God forbid, children. His own childhood had been messed up enough to turn him off the idea for life. Even if he did want a relationship, she was still his employee. And Artem was *not* his father, recent behavior notwithstanding.

But sitting an arm's length away from Ophelia right now felt like torture. He felt anything but fine.

"I'd like to propose a new marketing campaign for the ballerina collection now that certain, ah, facts have come to light." Dalton nodded.

So he was going right in for the kill, was he? Artem's fists clenched even tighter.

"A new marketing campaign?" Ophelia's eyes went wide, and the panic Artem saw in their sapphire depths took the edge off his anger and softened it a bit. Changed it to something that felt more like sorrow. Deep, soul-shaking sorrow.

"Yes. I'm thinking a print campaign. Artful black-and-white shots, perhaps even a few television commercials, featuring you, of course."

"Me?" She swallowed, and Artem traced the movement up and down the slender column of her throat.

For a moment, he was transfixed. Caught in a memory of his mouth moving down Ophelia's neck. In his mind, he heard the soft shudder of a moan. He felt the tremulous beat of her pulse beneath his tongue. He saw a sparkling flash of diamonds against porcelain skin.

Then he blinked, and he was back in the conference room, with Ophelia appraising him coolly from the opposite side of the table.

If only Dalton weren't present. Artem would tell her exactly how enraged he felt about being ghosted. Or maybe he'd simply lay her down on the smooth oak surface of the table and use his mouth on her until she shattered.

Perhaps he'd do both those things.

But Dalton was most definitely there, and he was talking again. Going on about advertisements in the *Sunday Times* and a special catalog for the holidays. "You'll wear ballet shoes, of course. And a tutu."

Finally, *finally*, Ophelia looked at Artem. Really looked at him. If he'd thought he'd caught a glimpse of brokenness in her gaze before he'd known about her MS, it would have been unmistakable now. Somewhere in the sapphire depths of her gaze, he saw a plea. Someone needed to put a stop to what was happening.

The things Dalton was proposing were out of the question. How could his brother fail to understand that dressing the part of what she could no longer be would kill Ophelia? Artem could almost hear the sound of her heart breaking.

He cleared his throat. "Dalton…"

But his brother wasn't about to be dissuaded so easily. Clearly, he'd been mulling over new marketing strategies all weekend. "You'll wear the Drake Diamond, of course. I'd like to get it reset in your tiara design as soon as possible. You'll be the face of Drake Diamonds. Your image will be on every bus and in every subway station in New York. Possibly even a billboard in Times Square. Now I know you haven't performed in a while, but if you could dance for just a bit, just long enough to tape a commercial segment, we'd be golden."

Artem couldn't believe his ears. Now Dalton was asking Ophelia to dance? No. Just no. Ballet was special to her. Far too special to be exploited, even if it meant saving Drake Diamonds. Maybe Dalton wasn't capable of understanding just what it meant to her, since he'd never seen her dance. But Artem had.

He knew. He knew what it felt like to go breathless at the sight of her arabesque. He knew how just the sight of her arched foot could cause a man to ache with longing. Artem would carry that knowledge to his grave.

And Dalton expected her to dance for him? In a television commercial, of all things?

Ophelia would never agree to it. Never. Even if she did, Artem wouldn't let her.

Over his dead fucking body.

Ophelia did her best to look at Dalton and focus on what he was saying, as ludicrous and terrifying as it was, but he was beginning to look a bit blurry around the edges.

Not now. Please not now.

She hadn't even managed to get back to her own apartment on Saturday morning before her MS symptoms began to make themselves felt. She'd taken a cab rather than the subway, afraid of being spotted in public in her ball gown from the night before. The same ball gown she was wearing on the front page of the morning newspaper. As she'd sat in the backseat of the taxi, biting her lip and staring at the snow swirling out the window while she'd tried not to cry, she'd felt a strange numbness creeping over her.

It had started with her fingertips. Just a slight tingling sensation, barely noticeable at first. She'd stared down at her hands, clutching the pointe shoes she'd almost left behind, and realized she was shaking. That's when she'd known.

She'd been unable to stop the tears when she realized she'd become symptomatic. Fate hadn't exactly been kind to her lately, but this seemed impossibly cruel. Too cruel to believe. Her lips had still been swollen from Artem's kisses, her body still warm from his bed. Why did it have to happen then? Why?

Logically, she knew the answer. Stress.

The doctors had been clear in the beginning— stress could make her condition worse. Even a perfectly healthy body responded to stress, and as Ophelia was only too aware, her body was neither perfect nor healthy. Her medical team had counseled her to build a life for herself that was as stress-free as possible, which was why she'd begun volunteering at the animal shelter. And one of the multitude of reasons why she'd never considered dating. Or even contemplated the luxury of falling in love.

She'd slipped. Once. Only once.

For a single night, she'd forgotten she was sick. She'd allowed herself to live. Really live. And now her life, her secrets, everything she held dear, was front-page news. Something to read about over morning coffee.

All of that would have been stressful enough without the added heartbreak of knowing that Artem would see those words and that he'd never look at her the same way again. Never see her with eyes brimming with desire rather than pity.

It was no wonder her fingertips had gone numb. No wonder she'd fallen down when she'd exited the cab. No wonder the tingling sensation had only gotten worse when Artem had shown up at her apartment and practically beaten down the door, while she'd curled in the fetal position on the sofa with Jewel's tiny, furry form pressed to her chest.

She'd wished then that the numbness would overtake her completely. That it would spread from her fingers and toes, up her arms and legs, until it reached her heart. She wished she could stop feeling what she felt for him.

She missed him.

She missed him with an intensity that frightened her.

So the blurry vision really should have come as no surprise as she sat across from Artem in the Drake Diamonds conference room and listened to his brother's horrifying idea for promoting her jewelry collection.

Dalton wanted her to dance. On television.

"No," Artem said. Calmly. Quietly. But the underlying lethality in his tone was impossible to ignore.

"I beg your pardon?" Dalton said, resting his hands on the conference table.

"You heard me."

Dalton cast a tense smile in Ophelia's direction. "I think the choice is Ophelia's, Artem."

Ophelia cleared her throat. She suddenly felt invisible, which should have been a relief. But there was something strangely disconcerting about the way Artem studiously avoided her gaze, even as he came to her rescue.

Why was he doing this, even after she'd refused to take his calls or see him? She didn't know, and thinking about it made her heart hurt.

"That's where you're wrong, brother. The choice isn't hers to make because there *is* no choice. We're not doing the campaign. We're not resetting the Drake Diamond. It's going up for auction three weeks from today."

Wait. *What?*

Dalton let out a ragged sigh. "Tell me the contract hasn't been signed. Tell me it's not too late to undo this."

Artem shrugged as if they were discussing something as banal as what to order for lunch rather than a priceless gem that glittered with family history. Both his and hers. "The papers are on my desk awaiting my signature, but I'm not changing my mind. Ophelia will not wear your tiara, and neither will she dance in your ad campaign."

Silence fell over the room, so thick that Ophelia could hardly breathe.

She shook her head and managed to utter a single syllable. "Don't."

"Don't?" Artem turned stormy eyes on her. "Are you telling me you actually *want* to go along with this marketing strategy?"

"That's not what I'm saying at all." She slid her gaze to Dalton. "Dalton, I'm sorry. I can't. Won't, actually."

She'd needed to say it herself. The truth of the matter was she didn't need Artem to fight her battles. She could—and *should*—be fighting them herself.

She might be on the brink of a relapse, but she could still speak for herself and make her own decisions. Besides, Artem wouldn't always be there to take her side, would he? In fact, she couldn't figure out why in the world he was trying to protect her now. Other than the obvious—he felt sorry for her. Pity was the absolute last thing she wanted from him.

Exactly what do *you want from him?*

So many things, she realized, as a lump formed in her throat. Maybe even love.

Stop.

She couldn't allow herself to think that way. Despite his wealth and power, the man had obviously had a tumultuous emotional life. Could she really expect him to take on a wife who would certainly end up a burden?

Wife? *Wife?* Since when had she allowed herself to even fantasize about marriage? She needed to have her head examined.

"I don't understand." Dalton frowned.

"There's nothing to understand. You heard Miss Rose. She isn't dancing, and the diamond is going up for auction. Case closed." Artem stood and buttoned his suit jacket, signaling the meeting was over.

How was everything happening so fast?

"Wait," Ophelia said.

She'd lost her family. And her health. And ballet.

And she'd never have Artem, the only man she'd ever wanted.

But she would *not* lose the Drake Diamond. She

knew Artem would never understand. How could he? But that diamond—that *rock*, as he so frequently called it—was her only remaining connection to her family.

She would never marry. Never have children. Once she was gone, the Baronova name would be nothing more than a memory. She could live with that. She could. But that knowledge would be so much easier to swallow if only something solid, something real, remained. A memory captured in the glittering facets of a priceless jewel. A jewel that generations of people would come to see. People would come and look at that diamond, and they would remember her family.

The Baronovas had lived. They'd lived, and they'd mattered.

"Please, Artem." Her voice broke as she said his name. She was vaguely aware of Dalton watching her with a curious expression, but she didn't care. "Don't sell the diamond. Please."

Her eyes never left Artem's, despite the fact that being this close to him and pretending the memory of their night together didn't haunt her with every breath she took was next to impossible. She'd had no idea how difficult it would be to see him in this context. To sit a chaste distance apart when she longed for his touch. To see the indifference in his gaze when she could all but still feel him moving inside her. It was probably the hardest thing she'd ever done in her life apart from hearing her diagnosis. Maybe even worse.

Because if she'd only taken his calls or answered the door when he'd pounded on it, he wouldn't be looking at her like that, would he? He wouldn't be so angry he couldn't look her in the eye.

"I'm sorry, Miss Rose." But he didn't sound sorry at all.

Then he focused on the floor, as if she was the last person in the world he wanted to see. In that heartbreaking moment, Ophelia understood that pity wasn't the worst thing she could have found in his gaze, after all.

"My mind is made up. This meeting is adjourned."

Chapter Ten

Ophelia was certain Artem would change his mind at some point in the weeks leading up to the auction. He couldn't be serious about selling the diamond. Worse, she couldn't understand why he'd made such a choice. And why didn't Dalton put up more of a fight to keep it in the family?

Granted, the decision was Artem's to make. He was the CEO. The Drake family business was under *his* leadership. Not that he took to the mantle of authority with enthusiasm. After all, he'd been set to resign on the day they'd met.

And now she thought she knew why.

I'm not really a Drake, Ophelia.

She got a lump in her throat every time she thought about the look in his eyes when he'd said those words.

Storm-swept eyes. Eyes that had known loss and longing. Eyes like the ones she saw every time she looked in the mirror.

She and Artem had more in common than she would ever have thought possible.

But if what was being printed in the newspapers was any indication, he had every intention of going through with the sale of the diamond. And why wouldn't he, since he clearly felt no sentimental attachment to it?

She did, though. And now Artem knew exactly how much that diamond meant to her. The fact that he apparently didn't care shouldn't have stung. But it did.

She hated herself for wishing things could be different. She'd slept with Artem. She'd thrown herself at him, naked in both body and soul, knowing it was for only one night. What had she thought would happen?

Not this.

Not the persistent ache deep in the center of her chest. Not the light-headed feeling she got every time she thought about him. Not the constant reminders everywhere she turned.

Artem's face was everywhere. On the television. On magazines. In the papers. Details of the auction were front-page news. Appraisers speculated about the purchase price. Most of them agreed the diamond would go for at least forty-five million. Probably more.

If there was a silver lining to the sale of the diamond, it was that in the excitement over the auction, *Page Six* had all but forgotten about Ophelia. Up until the press release, her photo had been in the paper every day. The paparazzi gathered outside her building and followed her to work in the morning. They followed her to the subway station. They even followed her to her volunteer shifts at the animal shelter. It was beyond unnerving. Ophelia lived in fear of losing her balance and being photographed facedown on the pavement. She knew that was what the photographers were waiting for. A disastrous stumble. A breakdown. An image that showed how far she'd fallen since her glory days as a promising ballerina. Something that would make the readers cry for her. With her.

She was determined not to give it to them. She'd lost Artem. And now she was losing the diamond. She refused to lose her dignity. It was all she had left.

But once news of the auction broke, the mob outside her door vanished. Overnight, she became yesterday's news.

She knew she should be grateful. Or at the very least, relieved. But it was difficult to feel anything but regret as days passed without so much as a word from Artem. Or even a glimpse of him.

He hadn't set foot inside Drake Diamonds since that awful Monday morning in the conference room. Three weeks of silence. Twenty-one days of absence that weighed on her heavier than a fur blanket.

Even on the lonely Friday morning when the armed guards from Sotheby's showed up to remove the Drake Diamond from its display case on the sales floor, Artem had been conspicuously absent. Ophelia couldn't bring herself to watch.

Not until the day of the auction did she finally come to accept that not only was Artem actually going through with the sale of the diamond, but he might never return to Drake Diamonds. She might never see him again. Which was for the best, really. Absolutely it was. She wasn't sure why the prospect made her feel so empty inside.

Because you're in love with him.

No.

No, she wasn't. She was in love with the way he'd made her feel. That was different, wasn't it? It had to be. Because she couldn't be in love. With anyone. Least of all, Artem Drake.

The auction was set to begin at noon sharp, and the store had set up an enormous television screen in the ground level showroom. Champagne was being served, along with platters of Drake-blue petits fours and rock candy in the shape of emerald cut diamonds. It was a goodbye party of sorts, and half of Manhattan had shown up.

Ophelia shut herself in her tiny office and tried to pretend it was a regular workday. Her desk was covered in piles of half-drawn sketches for the new collection she was designing to mirror the art deco motif of the Plaza. But losing herself in her work didn't even help, because Artem's absence was there, too. The memory of their night together lived in the glittering swirl of the pavé brooch she'd finally finished. The unbroken pattern of the diamonds mirrored the whirl of a midnight snowfall, and the inlaid amethysts were as pale pink as her ballet shoes.

Would it always be this way? Was she destined to live in the past? In the grainy black-and-white photos of her grandmother's tiara and in the jewels that told the story of the night she'd made what had probably been the biggest mistake of her life?

Her fingertips tingled and the pencil slipped out of her hand. She tore the sheet of paper from her sketchpad and crumpled it in a ball, but she couldn't even manage to do that properly. It fell to the floor.

Ophelia sat staring at it, and reality hit her. Hard and fast. This was her present. Right here. This moment. Dropping things. Feeling frustrated. Missing someone.

It would also be her future. Her future wouldn't be one of diamonds and dancing or making love while a snowstorm raged against the windows of Artem's penthouse in the sky. It wouldn't be ballet or music or the velvet hope of a darkened theater. Her future would be moments just like this one.

She should never have slept with him.

She'd done what she'd set out to do. She was a jewelry designer at the most prestigious diamond company in North America, if not the world. She'd reinvented herself.

And still, somehow, it wasn't enough.

Artem slipped out of Sotheby's once the bids exceeded twenty million dollars, the sum total of the Drake Diamonds deficit, thanks to dear old dad and his worthless Australian mine.

Ophelia's ballerina diamonds had brought in close to five million in under a month, which was remarkable. Sometimes Artem wondered if it would have been enough. If they'd only had more time.

If...

Artem had never been one to indulge in what-ifs. Since his night with Ophelia, he'd been plagued with them. What if he'd been able to warn her about the article on *Page Six* before she found it herself? What if he wasn't her boss? What if she wasn't sick?

What if he'd never agreed to sell the diamond?

But none of that mattered, did it? Because all those obstacles existed. Now he just wanted to forget. He wanted to forget Drake Diamonds. He even wanted to forget Ophelia. He would have done anything to erase the memory of the way he'd felt when he'd seen her dance. Spellbound. Captivated. And now that night haunted him.

He just wanted out. *Needed* out.

So the moment the bidding escalated and he knew that Drake Diamonds would live to see another day, he left. Walked right out the door, and no one even seemed to notice. Even the reporters gathered at the back of the room were focused so intently on the auctioneer, they didn't see him as he strode past. For the first time in weeks, he slid into the backseat of his town car without being photographed.

"Home, sir?" the driver asked, eyeing him in the rearview mirror.

Artem shook his head. "The store."

"Yes, sir."

It was time to put an end to things. For good.

As expected, the showroom was a circus. The auction was still in progress, apparently, so once again his presence went wholly undetected. Good. He'd go upstairs, leave his letter of resignation on Dalton's desk and set things right. He'd do what he should have done weeks ago, before he'd gotten so hopelessly distracted by Ophelia Baronova.

The tenth floor was a ghost town. For once, there wasn't a single pair of doe-eyed lovers in Engagements trying on rings over champagne and petits fours. Artem wasn't sure whether he found the heavy silence a relief or profoundly sad. Perhaps a little bit of both.

He wasn't sure why he glanced inside the kitchen as he walked past. Probably because that's where he'd first seen Ophelia, where everything had changed. With one look. One word. One tiny bite of cake.

His gaze flitted toward the room, and for a moment, he thought he was seeing things. There she was, in all her willowy perfection, surrounded by champagne flutes and petits fours just as she'd been all those weeks ago. As if somehow his desire had conjured her into being.

He blinked and waited for her image to shimmer and fade, as it always did. Since the night she'd spent in his bed, he'd been haunted. Tormented. She moved through the shadows of his penthouse in balletic apparitions. A ghost of a memory.

He'd intentionally stayed away from the store so he wouldn't be forced to look at her. But still he'd seen her everywhere. So he was almost surprised when she spoke to him, confirming that she was, in fact, real and not just another one of his fantasies.

She said one word. His name. "Artem."

Her voice faltered a little.

He glanced at the petit four in her hand. It trembled slightly, either from nerves or a by-product of her MS. An ache formed in the center of his chest.

He'd once enjoyed toying with Ophelia, rattling her, getting under her skin. That was before he'd seen her so boldly confident when she'd stood before him and let her dress fall to the floor. He wanted that Ophelia back. He didn't want to frighten her. He wanted her fearless and bold. He wanted her breathless. He wanted her bared.

He wanted her.

Still. He always would.

How could she possibly be sick? Time and again, he'd tried to wrap his mind around it. He'd read all the articles about her in the papers. He'd even Googled the coverage of her incident onstage—the sudden fall that had led to her diagnosis. No matter how many times he saw the words in print, he still couldn't bring himself to believe it. It just didn't seem possible that a woman who could dance the way Ophelia had danced for him could have a chronic medical condition. She'd moved with such breathless abandon. How could it be true?

That dance was all he could think about. Even now. *Especially* now, as he stood looking at her in the Drake Diamonds kitchen. Again.

This was where they'd begun. He supposed it was only fitting they should end here, as well.

He just needed to get in and get out, to at *long last* tender his resignation and never set foot in the building again. He'd done what he needed to do. He'd sold the diamond. He'd saved the company.

He wasn't needed at Drake Diamonds anymore. Dalton could take it from here. It's what his brother had always wanted, anyway, and Artem was only too happy to let him.

"We must stop meeting like this, Ophelia," he said, trying—and failing—not to look at her mouth.

"You're back." She sounded less than thrilled. Good. *Get mad, Ophelia. Feel something. Anything.*

He shook his head. "Not really."

She rolled her eyes. "Don't tell me you're quitting again."

"As a matter of fact, that's exactly why I'm here."

She lowered the petit four to the plate in her hand and set it down on the counter. "I was joking."

He shrugged. "I'm afraid I'm not."

How ridiculous that the last conversation they would ever have would be about business. It was absurd.

"You're quitting?" Her voice softened to almost a whisper, but somehow it still seemed to carry the weight of all the words they'd left unsaid. "Is this because..."

Every muscle in Artem's body tensed. "Don't say it, Ophelia." He did *not* want to discuss his illegitimacy. Not here. Not now. "I'm warning you. Don't go there."

"You're the one who should be running this company, Artem. It's your birthright, just as much as it is Dalton's." She rested her hand on his forearm. Her touch was as light as a butterfly, but it was nearly his undoing. If he stayed another minute, he would kiss her. Another five, and he'd be tempted to lay her across the kitchen table.

He shrugged her off. "We're not having this discussion."

"Fine. But you should at least talk to your brother about it before you do something ridiculous like resign."

"You're the last person who should be lecturing me about quitting," he said, knowing even as he did that he was taking things too far. He couldn't seem to make himself stop, though.

"What are you talking about? I'm not the one quitting my job." She jammed her pointer finger into his chest. "You are."

"You're right about that. I'm quitting my job." He crossed his arms. "But you, my darling, have quit everything else. You've quit life."

Her eyes glittered with indignation. "You don't understand."

"Make me, Ophelia. Make me understand." He reached for her hand, but she pulled away.

Then she threw his words right back at him. "We're not having this discussion."

"As you wish." He nodded.

This was better. Anger was better than ache. She didn't want to discuss her illness any more than he wanted to discuss his family history. They had nothing left to say to one another.

Other than goodbye.

He took a deep breath. *Just say it. Say the words. Goodbye, Ophelia.*

"Goodbye, Artem." She brushed past him with an indifference he would have envied if he'd bought it for even a second.

He turned to stop her just in time to see her stumble.

The world seemed to move in slow motion as she lost her footing and fell against the kitchen counter. Artem rushed to her side, but she gripped the counter instead of his arm. She righted herself, then refused to meet his gaze.

"Are you all right?" He regretted the words the moment they left his mouth.

Of course she wasn't all right. She was sick. Nothing about that was right.

"I'm fine," she snapped.

But she didn't look fine. Far from it. Her skin had gone ghostly pale. He had the strangest feeling that she wasn't altogether there. As if in the midst of a conversation, she might fade and disappear.

"Don't." She shook her head. "Do not ask me if I'm all right. And please don't look at me like that."

"Like what?" he prompted. He was looking at her the only way he knew how. Like he missed her.

Because by God, he did. He knew he shouldn't. But he did.

"Like you feel sorry for me. Like I'm this fragile, broken creature that needs to be fixed." She lifted her chin and finally looked him in the eye. "That's not how I want you to see me."

"Your illness is the last thing I see when I look at you, Ophelia. Surely you know that."

She blinked, but her eyes didn't seem to fully take him in.

Artem needed her to hear him. He needed her to understand that he didn't see her as a tragic waif, but as a balletic beauty. Desire personified. Nothing would ever change that. Not even the goodbye that was on the tip of his tongue.

"Artem," she whispered. "I think I…"

Her voice was the first thing to fade away, then her lovely sapphire eyes drifted shut and she fell unconscious into his arms.

Chapter Eleven

She had to be dreaming.

The heat of Artem's body, the rustle of his smooth wool suit jacket against her cheek, the sheer comfort of once again being in his arms…none of it could be real.

She had to be dreaming.

Ophelia fought the instinct to open her eyes. Railed against it. She wanted to linger here in the misty place between sleep and wakefulness, the place where she could dream and dance. The place where things hadn't gone so horribly wrong.

No matter how hard she tried, though, she couldn't seem to stop the sounds of the real world from pressing in—the ding of a bell, a familiar grinding noise and the soothing cadence of Artem's voice.

"Ophelia, wake up. Please wake up."

Her eyes fluttered open, and though things looked hazy, as if she were seeing them through a veil, the familiarity of Artem's chiseled features was unmistakable. Her heart gave a little lurch as she took in the angle of his cheekbones and the sureness of his square jaw.

He was so close she could have reached out and traced the handsome planes of his face with her fingertips, if only she could move. But her arms seemed impossibly heavy. And she couldn't feel her legs beneath her at all. She *wasn't* dreaming, but what on earth was happening?

"Ah, Sleeping Beauty. You've returned." Artem smiled down at her.

He was here. He was smiling. And, oh, God, he was *carrying* her in his strapping arms.

She managed to lift one hand and push ineffectively against his chest. His solid, swoon-worthy chest. "Put me down."

His smile faded, which did nothing to lessen the effect of his devastating good looks. If anything, he was more handsome when he was angry, which was wrong on so many levels.

"No," he growled.

"Artem, I'm serious." Why did her voice sound so slurred?

"As am I. You fainted, and now I'm taking you to the hospital."

Fainted? *Hospital?*

She heard another ringing sound and managed to tear her gaze away from Artem. She recognized the close quarters now—the neat row of numbered buttons, the dark wood paneling, the crystal chandelier overhead. They were standing in the posh elevator of Drake Diamonds. Correction—*Artem* was standing. She most definitely was not.

"Put me down. I'm not letting you carry me through the showroom and out the front door of the store." There were hundreds of people downstairs, including the media.

He glared down at her. "And have you faint on me again? No, thank you."

The fog in her head began to clear, and things started coming back into focus. She remembered sneaking off to the kitchen. It had been the first time she'd set foot in there since the day she'd met Artem. When would she learn her lesson? And just what did the universe have against her indulging in a tiny bit of cake every now and then?

But had it really been a coincidence? Or somewhere deep inside had she been hoping he would come?

"Artem, please." She fought the sob that was making its way up her throat. "The photographers."

His blue eyes softened a bit, and he lowered her gently to her feet. He kept a firm grip on her waist, though, and all but anchored her to his side. "Hold on to me while we walk to the car. My driver is meeting us at the curb."

She nodded weakly. She felt impossibly tired as the reality of what just happened came crashing down on her.

She'd fainted. At work.

She'd fainted only one other time in her life, and that

had been the day her dancing career had ended. Why was this happening again? She was relapsing. It was the only explanation. For weeks now, she'd been experiencing minor symptoms. She'd been so ready to chalk them up to stress. But this was serious. She'd passed out.

In front of Artem, of all people.

The elevator chimed as they reached the ground floor, and he pulled her closer against him. In the final moments before the elevator doors swished open, he took her hand and placed her arm around his waist, all but ensuring they looked like lovers rather than what they were.

What were they, anyway? Ophelia didn't even know.

The doors opened. She blinked against the dazzling lights of the showroom and stiffened, resisting the instinct to burrow into Artem's side.

He whispered into her hair, "Do not let go of me, Ophelia. If you try to walk out of here on your own, I'll turn you over my shoulder and carry you out caveman-style while every photographer in Manhattan snaps your photo. Understood?"

Her cheeks flared with heat. "Fine."

The man was impossible.

And no, she didn't understand. Why was he doing this? Why didn't he just call an ambulance and let the paramedics carry her away on a stretcher? Surely he wasn't planning on actually accompanying her all the way to the hospital? When she'd fainted midperformance at the ballet, not one person had ridden with her to the ER. Not even Jeremy.

She kept her gaze glued to the floor as Artem escorted her across the showroom, through the rotating doors and onto the snowy sidewalk. Beside her, he spoke politely—charmingly even—to the photographers as the shutters on their cameras whirred and clicked. At first she didn't understand why. Then she realized he was putting on a show, distracting them from what was really going on. Everyone would think they were a couple now, but at least she wouldn't look sick and vulnerable in front of the entire world.

The press peppered him with questions. At first, they didn't make sense. Then, as she looked around, she realized what had happened. While she and Artem had been arguing in the kitchen, the auction had ended.

"Mr. Drake, do you have anything to say about the auction? Are you happy with the purchase price of fifty-six million?"

"How do you feel about the Drake Diamond moving to Mexico City?"

Mexico City? The diamond wouldn't even be in the country anymore.

Ophelia's knees began to grow weak as they approached the car. Artem's driver held the door open and she slid across the bench seat of the limousine. Artem followed right behind and eyed her with concern as she exhaled a deep breath and sank into the buttery leather.

Snowflakes swirled against the car windows and her heart suddenly felt like it could beat right out of her chest. This—Artem, the snow, the unexpected intimacy of the moment—stirred up every memory she'd been fighting so hard to repress, and brought them once again into sharp focus. She couldn't be here. Not with him. Not again.

"Artem." She would tell him to leave. To just go back inside and let the driver drop her off at the hospital. She'd be fine. She'd done this before all by herself. Why should this time be any different?

"Ophelia." He reached and cupped her cheek, and despite her best intentions, she let her head fall into the warmth of his touch.

She went liquid, as liquid as the sea, powerless to fight his pull. Because Artem was as beautiful as the moon, and whatever this was between them felt an awful lot like gravity.

"Thank you," she whispered.

Artem paced back and forth in Ophelia's hospital room, unable to sit still. At least he'd managed to get her immediately moved to a private room rather than the closet-sized space where they'd originally placed her. He'd walked in, taken a look around and marched right back out.

If she suspected his influence was behind her relocation to more acceptable surroundings, she didn't mention it. Then again, she wasn't exactly in fighting form at the moment. Case in point—she hadn't tried to kick him out of her room yet, which was for the best. Artem would rather avoid a nasty scene, and he had no intention of leaving her here. Alone.

She looked as beautiful as ever, asleep on the examination table with her waves of blond hair spilled on the pillow like spun gold. She looked like Sleeping Beauty, awaiting the kiss that would bring her back to life. The comparison brought an ache to Artem's gut.

She'd scared the hell out of him when she'd fainted. His heart had all but stopped the moment she slumped into his arms. He needed to know she was okay before he even thought about walking out the door.

Or out of her life.

But she wasn't okay. MS didn't simply go away. Artem could throw all the money he had at the situation, and it wouldn't do a bit of good. He'd never felt so helpless, so out of control, in his life. It didn't sit well. He'd thought he could fix this, if only she'd let him. Now he realized how very wrong he'd been.

The door opened, and a nurse in blue scrubs walked in. "Miss Rose?"

"She's sleeping," Artem said.

"I just have a few questions." The nurse smiled.

Artem did not.

They'd already listened to her heart, taken her pulse and filled up three vials with her blood. He was ready for answers or, at the very least, a conversation with an actual doctor.

He forced himself to quit pacing and stand still. "Is that really necessary?"

"I'm afraid so, Mr, ah…" She flipped through the folder in her hand until her gaze landed on a name. "…Davis."

Artem lifted a brow. "I beg your pardon. Who?"

"Miss Rose's emergency contact. Mr. Jeremy Davis. I'm sorry. I assumed that was you." She frowned down at the papers in her hand. Clearly, the staffers in the emergency room hadn't filled her in on Artem's identity, which probably would have irritated him if he hadn't been momentarily distracted by being called by another man's name. "Shall I give Mr. Davis a call?"

"No." Ophelia, awake now, sat bolt upright on the exam table. "Absolutely not. In fact, take his name off my paperwork."

Artem crossed his arms and regarded her as she studiously avoided his gaze.

The nurse made a few notes and then looked back up as her pen hovered over the page. "Whose name would you like to write down in place of Mr. Davis?"

"Um…" Ophelia cleared her throat. "Can we just leave that space blank for now? Please?"

The nurse shook her head. "I'm afraid we must have an emergency contact. It's hospital policy."

"Oh." Ophelia stared down at her lap. "In that case, um…"

"Allow me." Artem reached for the nurse's clipboard and pen.

"Artem, don't." Ophelia struggled to her feet.

"Sit. Down." His command came out more sternly than he'd intended, but he'd already had enough of a fright without watching her faint again and hitting her head on the hospital's tile floor.

Ophelia sat and fumed in silence while Artem finished scribbling his name and number, then thrust the clipboard back at the nurse. "Done. Now when can we talk to the doctor?"

He didn't want to think about why he thought it only proper that he should be Ophelia's emergency contact.

Nor did he want to contemplate the identity of Jeremy Davis. He just wanted to make Ophelia better.

What in the world was he doing? He'd never taken care of anyone in his life. He'd certainly never been anyone's emergency contact. Not even for his siblings. The truth of the matter was he'd carefully arranged his life in a way to avoid this kind of obligation. He'd had enough of those. He'd been an obligation his entire life—the child the Drakes had accepted because they'd had to. It was easier to remain entirely self-contained.

Except Ophelia didn't feel like a chore. She felt more like a need he couldn't quite understand.

This wasn't him.

"The doctor will be by any minute. We're just waiting on some test results from the lab." The nurse turned her attention back to Ophelia. "Can you tell me more about your symptoms? Have you been experiencing any dizziness before this morning?"

Ophelia nodded. "A little."

This was the moment he should leave. Or at the very least, step into the hallway. He'd delivered Ophelia to the hospital. He'd seen to it that she would have the best care money could buy. But in reality, her health was none of his business.

He glanced at her, fully expecting to be given his marching orders. She'd certainly never minced words with him before, which made it all the more poignant when she said nothing, but instead looked back at him with eyes as big as saucers.

She was afraid.

She was afraid, and if he left her now, she'd be sitting

in this sterile room in her flimsy paper gown, waiting for bad news all alone.

Artem felt an odd stirring in his chest. He sat beside her on the examination table and took her hand in his.

The nurse pressed on with more questions. "Any other problems associated with your MS? Tingling? Numbness?"

"Yes." Beside him, Ophelia swallowed. "And yes. In my hands mostly."

Artem stared down at their interlocked fingers. He'd had no idea she'd become symptomatic. Then again, since their night together he'd seen her only once—at that awkward meeting in the conference room.

"And how long has this been going on?" the nurse asked.

"Three weeks ago last Saturday," she said, with an unmistakable note of certainty in her tone.

Three weeks ago last Saturday. The morning after. That dark winter morning when everything had spun so wildly out of control.

Shit.

Artem felt like pummeling somebody. Possibly himself. The nurse gathered more information, but he could barely concentrate on what was being said. When she'd finally filled what seemed like a ream of paper with notes, she flipped her folder closed and left the room.

Before the door even clicked shut behind her, Ophelia cleared her throat. Artem knew what was coming before she said the words.

"You don't have to stay. I mean, thank you for everything you've done. But I understand. You don't want to be here, and that's fine. I don't blame you." She let out a laugh. "I don't want to be here myself."

"Stop," he said.

"What?"

He reached for her chin, held it in place and forced her to look at him. "Stop telling me how I feel. I'll leave when I'm good and ready. Not a minute before. Understood?"

She narrowed her gaze and prepared to argue, which he'd fully expected. Things that had perplexed and frustrated him before were beginning to make more sense—her reluctance to adopt the kitten, her abrupt announcement on the first day she'd set foot in his penthouse that she didn't have relationships. Or sex. Something...or some*one*...had convinced Ophelia that having a medical condition meant she had to close herself off from the rest of the world. He could see it now, as clear and sharp as a diamond.

Of course, that made it no less frustrating.

"I—" she started.

He cut her off, ready to get to the crux of the matter. "Who is Jeremy Davis?"

She lifted an irritated brow. He'd struck a nerve. Good. An angry Ophelia was far preferable to a frightened Ophelia.

"He's the director of the ballet company," she said primly.

"*And* your emergency contact?" he prompted, noting—to his complete and utter horror—how very much he sounded like a jealous boyfriend.

"Yes." She waited a beat, then added, "And my former fiancé."

"Fiancé?" Now he didn't just sound like a jealous boyfriend. He felt like one, too. Except he didn't have any claim on Ophelia. He had no right at all to these unwelcome feelings that had taken hold of him.

He wasn't sure why people called it the green-eyed monster. While indeed monstrous, there was nothing green about it. His mood was as black as ebony. "What happened? Why didn't you marry him?"

"Isn't it obvious?" She gestured toward their sterile surroundings. "It was for the best, really. I didn't love him. I thought I did, but it wasn't love. I know that now."

If the idiot named Jeremy Davis had been standing beside them, Artem would have given the man a good reason to make use of the hospital's facilities. He didn't need to know what Ophelia's former fiancé had said or what, exactly, he'd done. He didn't need to know anything else at all, frankly. The truth was written all over Ophelia's face. It showed in the way she locked herself away from the world.

He'd hurt her.

Maybe Ophelia's biggest problem wasn't her MS. Maybe it was her past.

Yet another thing they had in common.

"I'm sorry," he whispered, and gave her hand a tender squeeze.

"For what?" The quaver in her voice nearly slayed him.

"For everything."

He meant it. Every damn thing. He was sorry for not

trying harder to reach her after the news of her medical condition became a front-page story. He was sorry he hadn't forced her to see him. He was sorry for selling the diamond, when he knew how much it meant to her. He should have found a way to keep it, to let her hold on to just one thing.

But most of all he was sorry for every bad thing that had ever happened to her. He was sorry for the past, both hers and his, and the way it seemed to overshadow everything. Never had he wanted so badly to let it all go.

The door swung open. A woman in a white coat entered and extended her hand toward Ophelia. "Miss Rose, I'm Dr. April Larson."

"Hello." She shook the doctor's hand and gestured toward Artem. "This is Artem Drake, my, ah…"

"Emergency contact," he said, and smiled.

"Wonderful. It's great to meet you both." Dr. Larson sat on the stool facing them and spread a folder open on her lap. "So, Ophelia. You had a fainting spell this morning? How are you feeling now?"

Beside him, Ophelia took a deep breath. "A little tired, actually."

Dr. Larson nodded. "That's completely normal, given your condition."

"My condition. Right." She smiled, but it didn't reach her eyes.

The doctor nodded again. "I'm afraid so. You need to get some rest, Ophelia. And I would suggest that you avoid stress as much as possible. There's not much else we can do for you."

"I see. So it's that bad, is it? The symptoms I've been

experiencing and the fainting…" She blinked back tears. "I'm no longer in remission. I'm relapsing. This is only the beginning. It's going to get worse, much worse. Just like last time. I'm on the verge of a full-blown MS attack. Is that what's happening?"

"What?" The doctor leaned forward and placed a comforting hand on her knee. "No, not at all."

Ophelia shook her head. "I don't understand."

But Artem did.

The godforsaken past was repeating itself. And this time, it was all his doing. He had no one to blame but himself. It wasn't enough to sit at his father's desk and run his father's company. How had he let this happen? How had he actually allowed himself to become the man he most despised?

The doctor smiled. *Don't say it. Do* not. "You're not relapsing, Ophelia. You're pregnant."

Chapter Twelve

Pregnant?

Ophelia couldn't believe what she was hearing. There had been a mistake. Of course there had. She couldn't possibly be pregnant.

With *Artem's* child.

She couldn't even bring herself to look at him. He'd gone deadly silent beside her. She could feel the tension rolling off him in waves. She wished he were somewhere else. *Anyplace* else, so she could have had an opportunity to figure out how and when to tell him. Or *if* she would have told him.

But she would have. Of course she would. Having someone's child was too important to keep secret.

A child.

She couldn't have a child! "But I'm on birth control

pills. I've been on them since my diagnosis. My primary physician said there was evidence that the hormones in oral contraceptives helped delay the onset of certain MS symptoms."

She'd never imagined she'd use them for actual birth control. But still. They were called *birth control pills* for a reason, weren't they?

Dr. Larson eyed Ophelia over the top of her glasses. "Did your primary doctor also tell you that your MS medications could decrease the effectiveness of oral contraceptives?"

"No." Of course not. She would have remembered an important detail like that. Or would she? She'd decided never to have sex again. And if she'd stuck to that decision—as she so clearly should have—that detail wouldn't have been so important. It wouldn't have mattered at all.

She dropped her head in her hands. "I don't know. It's possible. I hadn't planned on—" Goodness, this was mortifying. How could she have this discussion with Artem right here, seething quietly beside her? "—meeting anyone."

"Well, the heart has its own ideas, doesn't it? Congratulations." Dr. Larson smiled and shot a wink in Artem's direction. "To you both."

Obviously, the doctor had seen past Artem's introduction as her emergency contact and detected there was something more between them. Even though there wasn't. Other than the fact that he was apparently the *father of her unborn child.*

Ophelia felt faint again, but this time she knew it was

just psychological. She'd been so sure she was relapsing. She almost wished she were. How could she possibly raise a child? And what about the physical demands of pregnancy? Could she even do this?

According to what the doctor was saying, yes. Of course she could. She was even talking about how pregnancy frequently eased MS symptoms. Women with MS had children every day. Dr. Larson was going on about how having children was a leap of faith for anyone, and there was no reason why she shouldn't have a healthy, loving family.

Except there was. Two months ago, Ophelia couldn't bring herself to adopt a kitten. And now she was supposed to have a family? She was supposed to be someone's *mother* when she was terrified that one day she wouldn't even be able to take care of herself?

She didn't hear another word the doctor said. It was too much to wrap her mind around. She felt sick to her stomach. What was she going to do? Could she raise a baby? All on her own?

A baby changed everything. How could she have been so incredibly foolish? She'd wanted one night with Artem.

Just one.

But that wasn't altogether true, was it? She wasn't sure when it had happened—maybe when he'd kissed her hand after she'd danced for him, when he'd whispered the words she so desperately needed to hear. *Ophelia, you* are *a dancer*. The exact moment no longer mattered, but sometime on that snowy night she'd begun to want more. More life. More everything. But most of all, more of *him*.

"Ophelia."

She blinked. Artem was standing now, holding all her paperwork in one hand and cupping her elbow with his other.

"Let's go, kitten." He smiled. But it was a sad smile, one that nearly tore her heart in two.

What had she done?

"I didn't do this on purpose," she said, once they were settled in the backseat of his town car. "I promise."

"I know." His tone was calm. Too calm. Too controlled, given the fact that the set of his jaw looked hard enough to cut diamonds. "I know it all too well."

She nodded. "Good."

Artem's driver glanced over his shoulder as the car pulled away from the curb. "To the Plaza, sir?"

"No." Artem shook his head. Thank goodness. Ophelia had no intention of accompanying him back to his penthouse. Or anywhere. She needed a little time and space to come to grips with her pregnancy and figure out what she was going to do. "City hall, please."

City hall?

She slid her gaze toward Artem. "Have you got a parking fine you need to take care of or something?"

"No, I do not," he said. Again, in that eerily placid tone he'd adopted since they'd left the hospital. "You're an intelligent woman. You know very well why we're stopping at city hall."

Ophelia stared at him in disbelief. Surely he didn't expect her to marry him. Here. Now. Without even so much as a discussion about it. Or a proposal, for that matter. "I'm afraid I don't."

"We're to be married, of course." He couldn't be serious. But he certainly looked it as he stared back at her, his gaze steely with determination. "Straight away."

The driver—usually the epitome of professional restraint—let out a little cough. Artem didn't seem to notice. Apparently, he was so laser focused on the idea of a wedding that other opinions didn't matter. Hers included.

A hot flush rose to her cheeks. "I'm not marrying you, Artem."

Marrying him was out of the question. He knew that. She'd told him in the beginning that she didn't have relationships. Of course, she'd also told him she didn't have sex.

But still.

Artem Drake could marry anyone he chose. He couldn't possibly want to marry her. This was about the pregnancy. *Not* her. And even if the prospect of having a baby terrified her more than she would ever admit, she wouldn't marry a man who didn't love her.

Even if that man was Artem. And even if the thought of being his wife made her heart pound hard in her chest, just like it did when she danced.

"Yes, you are," he said, as if their marriage was a foregone conclusion.

Our marriage. Something stirred inside Ophelia. Something that felt too much like love.

Stop. You cannot *consider this.*

"If you want a more formal affair, or even a church

wedding, we can do that later. Whatever and wherever you wish. Vegas, Paris, Saint Patrick's Cathedral. Your choice. We can plan it for next week, next month or even after our baby is born, if that's what you prefer." *Our baby.* Ophelia's throat grew tight. She couldn't seem to swallow. Or breathe. "But we are getting legally married at city hall. Today. Right now."

It would have been so easy to say yes, despite the fact that he'd ordered her to marry him rather than actually asking. And despite the fact that she still couldn't forget the things Jeremy had once said to her. *Burden. Too much to deal with...*

Marrying Artem would mean she would have help with the baby. She wouldn't have to face her questionable future all alone. None of that mattered, though. The only thing that did was that marrying him would mean she could pledge her heart, her soul, her life to the man she loved.

She loved him. There was no more denying it. She'd loved him since the moment he'd seen past the wall she'd constructed around her heart and forced a kitten on her. Maybe even before then.

She loved him, and that's exactly why she couldn't marry him.

"Artem, please don't." She fixed her gaze out the window on the snowy blur of the city streets. She couldn't bring herself to look at him. Why was this so hard? Why did she have to fall in love? "I can't."

"Ophelia, I will not father a child out of wedlock. That is unacceptable to me. Please understand." He reached for her hand and squeezed it. Hard. Until she finally tore her gaze from the frosted glass and looked him in the eyes, the tortured windows to his soul. "Please."

His voice had dropped to a ragged whisper. A crack in his carefully measured composure. At last… That look, coupled with that whisper, nearly broke her.

Please understand.

She did. She understood all too well. She understood that Artem didn't want his baby to grow up without a father. His desire to get married had more to do with his past than it did with her. He was offering her the world. Paris. London. He was offering her everything she wanted, with one notable exception.

Love.

He hadn't said a single word about loving her. Maybe he did. But how could she possibly know that if he didn't tell her? And this ache she felt—the longing for him that seemed to come from deep in the marrow of her bones—was so intense it was dangerous. Desperate. Could something so wholly overwhelming possibly be reciprocated?

Because if it wasn't, if this was unrequited love, and Artem wanted to marry her out of obligation to their child, or as a way of mending his past, what would happen when her MS became worse? What would happen if she was one of the unlucky ones, one of the patients who ended up severely disabled? What then? If he loved her, they could get through it. Maybe. But if he didn't…

If he didn't, she would be a burden. Just as Jeremy had predicted. Artem would grow to resent her, and the thought of that frightened her even more than trying to raise a child by herself.

It would never work.

"I'm sorry." She shook her head and tried her best to maintain eye contact, but she just couldn't. She focused on the perfect knot in his tie instead. It grew blurry as she blinked back tears. *Say it. Just say it before you break down.* "I can't marry you, Artem. I can't, and I won't."

Chapter Thirteen

Artem sat seething across the desk from Dalton, unable to force thoughts of Ophelia and their unborn child from his mind. Fourteen hours and half a bottle of Scotch hadn't helped matters. If anything, he was more agitated about the unexpected turn of events than he'd been the night before.

She'd said no.

He'd asked Ophelia to marry him, and she'd said no. Rather emphatically, if memory served.

I can't marry you, Artem. I can't, and I won't.

"What's this?" Dalton asked, staring down at the envelope Artem slid toward him.

My long overdue letter of resignation. His personal life might be in a shambles at the moment, but he was determined to end the farce of his reign as CEO of

Drake Diamonds. At least that's why he told himself he'd come into the office today. If it had been to ask Ophelia to marry him—*again*—he would have been out of luck, anyway. Her office door had remained firmly closed for the duration of the morning.

Artem nodded at the letter. "Just read it."

Why should he disclose the contents when Dalton would know what the letter said as soon as he opened it? *If* he opened it.

"Whatever it is can wait," he said calmly. *No. No, it can't.* "There's a matter we need to discuss."

Dalton tossed the sealed envelope on his desk, opened the top drawer and pulled out a neatly folded newspaper. Artem sighed and closed his eyes for a moment. He knew what was coming before he even opened them and found Dalton leaning back in his chair, waiting for some sort of explanation. As if there could possibly be a plausible excuse for the photographs of him and Ophelia entwined with one another as they climbed into the car the day before.

"Well?" Dalton tapped with his pointer finger the copy of *Page Six* spread open on the desk.

Artem gave the paper a cursory glance. He didn't like looking at the picture. Seeing it reminded him of how he'd felt watching Ophelia fall, lifeless, into his arms. Powerless. Stricken.

Artem sighed. "What is your question, exactly?"

He had no desire to beat around the bush. The past twenty-four hours had been a godforsaken mess, and he was fresh out of patience.

I can't marry you, Artem. I can't, and I won't.

Why couldn't he get those words out of his head?

Dalton cleared his throat. "For starters, is the caption correct? Was this photo taking *during* the auction, when you were supposed to be at Sotheby's?"

At that moment, if Artem hadn't been the CEO, he might have begged to be fired. But alas, he couldn't be terminated. Much to his chagrin, he was untouchable.

"Yes." There wasn't a hint of apology in his voice. If anything, that simple syllable contained a thinly veiled challenge.

His mood was black enough to be ripe for a fight. At least if Dalton was his opponent, he'd have a decent chance of winning. Because Ophelia had shown no sign of surrender. After refusing to marry him, she'd asked the driver to drop her off at her apartment, and had all but ran inside in order to get away from Artem.

She wasn't going to get away with ghosting him again. Not when she was pregnant with his child. She would talk to him before the day's end. He'd seen to that already.

"I suppose it doesn't matter. The auction was successful." Dalton stared at the picture again, then lifted a brow at Artem. "But you're sleeping with Ophelia. That much is obvious. While you were away on your latest disappearing act, she started designing another collection. It's good. Brilliant, actually. The auction pulled us out of the red, but we need her."

Artem shifted in his chair. *We need her. I need her.* "It's not what you think, brother."

"Not what I think?" Dalton let out a laugh. "So you're not sleeping with her?"

"I didn't say that."

Another sigh. "Have you thought about what will happen when you get bored and still have to work with her every day?"

Bored? Not likely. Not when she had a certain knack for driving him to the brink of madness. In his bed, as well as out of it. "She's pregnant."

Why hide it? If he got his way, she'd be living under his roof within hours. Months from now, she'd be giving birth to his son or daughter. He'd never wanted to be a father, never even imagined it. But that no longer mattered. Artem had every intention of being a doting dad.

Marriage or no marriage.

The set of his jaw hardened, as it always did when he thought back on her trembling refusal. *I can't. I won't.*

"Pregnant?" Dalton paused. "With *your* child?"

Artem's mood grew exponentially blacker. "Of course the child is mine."

"Sorry, give me a minute. I'm still trying to wrap my head around this. Given our family past..." Dalton cleared his throat. Artem had to give him credit for choosing his words delicately, rather than just coming out and saying what they were both thinking. *Given the fact that you're my bastard brother...* "I'm surprised you weren't more careful."

So was Artem, to be honest. He'd never bedded a woman without wearing a condom. Never. Until Ophelia. But nothing about that night had been ordinary. The music, the ballet, the snow. The way he'd forgotten how to breathe when he'd seen her bare body for the first time.

It had been a miracle he'd remembered his own name, never mind a condom. "This was different. *She's different.*"

Dalton eyed him with blatant curiosity. "How, exactly?"

Because I love her.

By God, he did. He loved her. That's why he'd insisted on signing that emergency contact form before he'd even known she was pregnant. It's why he hadn't been able to work, sleep or even think since the morning she'd disappeared from his bed. It's why he wanted so very badly to take care of her. To make love to her again. And again.

To marry her.

It wasn't just the baby. It was *her.*

Artem cleared his throat and tried to swallow the realization that he was in love. With the mother of his child. With the woman who'd made it clear she had no intention of marrying him.

"My God, you're in love with her, aren't you?" Dalton said, as if he'd somehow peered right inside Artem's head.

"I didn't say that." But it was a weak protest. Even Artem realized as much the moment the words left his mouth.

"You don't have to. It's obvious." Dalton shrugged one shoulder. "To me, anyway."

Artem narrowed his gaze. It hadn't been obvious to himself until just now. Or maybe it had, and he hadn't wanted to believe it. "How so?"

"If you didn't love her, you would have never allowed this to happen. It's simple, really."

Artem wished things were simple. He'd never wished for anything as much. "You give me far too much credit, brother. Why don't you go ahead and say what we're both thinking?"

Dalton's gaze grew sharp. Pointed. "What is it I'm thinking?"

"The truth. I've become our father." No matter how many times he'd thought it, believed it, Artem felt sick saying it aloud. Like reality was a vile, dark malady crushing his lungs, stealing his breath.

Dalton looked at him for a long, silent moment before he finally replied. "That couldn't be further from the truth, brother. In fact, it might be the biggest load of bullshit I've ever heard."

If Dalton had ever been the type to humor him, Artem would have taken his reaction with a grain of salt. But Dalton hadn't been that sort of brother. Ever. If anything, Dalton had been hard on him, with his sarcastic comments about Artem's lavish lifestyle and what Dalton considered to be his less-than-stellar work ethic. As if any normal person's work ethic could compare to his workaholic brother's.

No, Dalton didn't make a practice of mincing words, but what he was saying made no sense. "Think about it. I've done exactly what Dad did. I had a fling with an employee, and now she's pregnant."

It was a crude way of putting it, and in truth, it didn't feel at all like what had happened. But it was, wasn't it?

No. It was more. It had to be.

Dalton shook his head. "You're forgetting something. Dad was married with two kids, and you are most assuredly not."

He had a point.

Still…

"I just can't believe this has all happened right after I stepped into his place here at the office. It's like he knew something I didn't." Artem dropped his head in his hands. "It should have been you, Dalton."

Dalton wanted to run the company. Artem didn't. He never had. He hated that he'd been the one chosen. Worse, he hated thinking their father had done it on purpose. That he'd known how alike they really were.

Like father, like son.

"No," Dalton said quietly. "It should have been you. It *had* to be you. Don't you get it?"

Artem lifted his head and met his brother's gaze. "*What? No.*"

"*Yes.* Dad knew he was sick, Artem. He also knew about the mine."

This was news to Artem. "You mean he knew it was worthless before he died?"

Dalton nodded. "The accountant confirmed it last week. If you'd bothered to show up at the office before now, I would have told you."

"I was trying to keep my distance from Ophelia." He'd thought he could get her out of his system. What a waste of time that had been. "He knew about the mine. What does that have to do with me?"

"*Everything.* It has everything to do with you. Dad knew the only way to save the company was to sell the diamond, and he knew I'd never do it. Hell, he couldn't even do it himself, otherwise he would have arranged for its sale as soon as he knew the mine was worthless."

Artem let this news sink in for a moment. Dalton was right. Their father never would have auctioned off the diamond. To him, it would have been like selling his family heritage. Worse, it would have been an admission that he'd failed. He'd failed the company and the long line of Drakes that had come before him.

Artem didn't give a damn about the long line of Drakes. Or the diamond. He didn't give a damn about being CEO. Ophelia was the only reason he'd stuck around as long as he had.

"You were the only one who would do it," Dalton said. "That's why he chose you, Artem. He didn't appoint you because he thought you were like him. He appointed you as CEO because you weren't like him at all."

Artem concentrated on breathing in and out while he processed what his brother was saying. He wanted to believe Dalton's theory. He wanted to believe it with everything in his soul.

"Listen to me, brother. What you did saved the company," Dalton said.

"It also helped push Ophelia away. That diamond meant something to her." He could still hear the desperation in her voice that day in the conference room. *Please, Artem. Don't sell the diamond. Please.* He hadn't listened.

He'd told himself he was doing the right thing. He'd been trying to put a stop to Dalton's ridiculous ad campaign. He'd been trying to protect her.

Maybe he had. But he'd also hurt her in the process. And now there was no going back.

"The fact remains that you saved the family business, and that makes you more of a Drake than anybody. More than me. More than Dad."

Artem wished he could take comfort in those words. There was a time when hearing Dalton say such a thing would have been a balm. Those words may have been all the healing he'd needed. Before.

Before Ophelia. Without her, they meant nothing. *He* meant nothing.

"About this." Dalton picked up the envelope containing Artem's letter of resignation. "Is this what I think it is?"

"It's my notice that I intend to step down as CEO," Artem said.

Dalton tore it neatly in half without bothering to open it. "Unaccepted."

For crying out loud. Could one thing go as planned? Just one? "Dalton…"

"Think on it for a while. Think about the things I've said. You may change your mind. The position pays awfully well."

As if Artem needed more cash. "I don't care about the money. I have plenty."

"You sure about that? After all, soon you'll have another mouth to feed." Dalton smiled, as if jumping at the chance to become a doting uncle.

A child. He and Ophelia were having a *child*. He'd been so stunned at the news, so abhorred by the idea that he'd become his father, that he hadn't realized how happy he was.

Ophelia was having his baby. That's all that mattered now. That, and convincing her to speak to him again. But he already had that covered.

"Think on it," Dalton said again. "I like having you around. It's about time we Drakes stuck together."

Ophelia blinked against the swirling snow and pulled her scarf more tightly around her neck as she stalked past the doorman of the Plaza, who was dressed, as usual, in a top hat and dark coat with shiny gold buttons. After hiding out in her office all day specifically to avoid facing Artem, she couldn't believe she was willingly setting foot in the hotel where he lived.

But he'd given her no choice, had he? He infuriated her sometimes. He had since the very beginning. But now…now he'd gone too far.

"Welcome to the Plaza." The concierge smiled at her, then before she even told him who she was, handed her a familiar-looking black key card, plus another, slimmer card. *Odd.* "The black card will give you access to the penthouse elevators and the other is the key to Mr. Drake's suite. He's expecting you."

I'll bet he is.

"Thank you." She did her best to smile politely. After all, the concierge had nothing to do with this ridiculous situation.

Or maybe he did. Who knew? Even Artem couldn't have pulled off a stunt like this without help.

And what was with the key to his suite? That had to

be a mistake. No way was she going to walk into his penthouse without knocking first. Although she supposed she was entitled, after what he'd done.

The elevator ride felt excruciatingly slow. Since arriving home from work and realizing what had happened, she hadn't stopped to think. She'd simply reacted. Which was no doubt what Artem had been counting on.

Now that she was moments away from seeing him again, she was nervous. Which was silly, really. She was having the man's baby. She should at least be able to carry on a simple conversation with him.

That was the trouble, though, wasn't it? Her feelings for Artem were anything but simple.

Yes, they are. You love him. Plain and simple.

She swallowed. That might be true, but it didn't mean she had to act on it. Or, God forbid, say it. But what *would* she say to him after refusing to marry him? And how could she see him again, so soon? She'd kept her office door closed all day for a reason. She didn't think she could take being in the same room with him without being able to touch him, to kiss him, to tell him how hard it had been to refuse him yesterday.

To pretend she didn't love him.

She'd told herself she'd done the right thing. Just because they were having a baby didn't mean they should get married. No matter how badly one of them wanted to.

She'd started to wonder, though, which one of them really wanted marriage. In her most honest moments, she realized it was her.

She didn't know what to do with these feelings. Everything had been so much easier when she'd kept to herself, when she'd gone straight home after work every day. No kitten. No nights at the ballet. No Artem.

Was it better then? Was it really?

At last the elevator reached the eighteenth floor, and Ophelia stepped into the opulent hallway. When she reached the door to penthouse number nine, she pounded on it before she had time to chicken out.

Artem opened it straightaway and greeted her with a devastating smile that told her she'd played right into his hand, just as she'd suspected. "Ophelia. Hello, kitten."

Her heart leaped straight to her throat, and to her complete and utter mortification, a ribbon of desire unfurled inside her. In an instant, her center went hot and wet.

She willed herself not to purr. "Kitten? Interesting choice of words, given the circumstances."

"Enlighten me. What would those circumstances be, exactly?" He crossed his arms and leaned casually against the door frame. Apparently, he was intent on making her go through the motions of this ludicrous charade.

"Artem, stop. You and I both know that you kidnapped my cat." She brushed past him into his suite, scanning the surroundings for a glimpse of Jewel.

Ophelia had been panicked when she'd come home from work and the little white fluffball hadn't greeted her at the door, winding around her ankles as she did every night. Then she'd seen the bouquet of white roses on the coffee table and Artem's business card propped against the lead crystal vase. No note. Just the card. *Artem Drake. Chief Executive Officer. Drake Diamonds.*

Chief Executive Ass was more like it.

Artem had broken into her apartment. He'd barged right in, and he'd stolen her cat.

"I beg your pardon. *Your* kitten?" He raised a sardonic brow. "As I recall, I'm the one who adopted her from the animal shelter when you refused to do so. That would make her *my* cat, would it not?"

No. Just...

No.

She looked over his shoulder and saw Jewel curled into a ball in the middle of his massive bed, right on top of the chinchilla blanket. The same blanket she'd wrapped around her naked self the last time she'd stood in this room. It was surreal. And possibly the most manipulative thing Artem Drake—or any other self-entitled male—had ever done.

"You can't be serious," she sputtered.

"Surely you remember how adamant you were about not adopting. I thought it best to relieve you of your cat-sitting responsibilities." He glanced at the kitten on the bed. "She rather likes it here. It's not such a bad place to be, Ophelia."

She heaved out a sigh and looked at Jewel. Memories of being in that same bed hit her, hard and fast. She envisioned herself waking up with her legs wrapped around Artem, her head nestled in the crook of his neck...

But wait, she wasn't actually considering letting him get away with this, was she? No. Of course she wasn't.

"Artem, you can't do this. I'm not marrying you, and if you think repossessing your kitten is going to change my mind, you're sorely mistaken."

"Who said anything about marriage? You don't want to marry me? Fine. I'm a big boy. I can take it." His tone went soft, sincere. The switch caught her off guard, and she felt oddly vulnerable all of a sudden. "But if you think I'm going to stand by and let you do this by yourself, you're the one who's mistaken. Let me be there for you, kitten. Let me take care of you. At least stay here."

"Stay here? With you?" She rolled her eyes.

"With me. Yes." There wasn't a hint of irritation in his tone. He'd dropped the overbearing act and was looking at her with such tenderness that her heart hurt.

Let me take care of you.

It was so close to *I love you* that it almost made her want to forgive him for breaking into her home. Seriously, who did that?

The man she was in love with. That's who.

"I shouldn't have come here." She shook her head and headed for the door.

She couldn't do this. If she stayed here for even one night, she'd end up back in his bed. And she'd never be able to leave him. Not again.

"Ophelia, stop. Please." Artem chased after her.

She shook her head. "I don't… I can't…"

He slid between her and the door, raised her chin with a gentle touch of his fingertips and forced her to look him in the eyes. "He was wrong, Ophelia. I don't know what Jeremy Davis said to you to make you believe that your MS made you unlovable, undesirable, but he was wrong. Dead wrong."

She took a few backward steps and wrapped her arms around herself in an effort to hold herself together. Because it felt like the entire world was falling to pieces around her. Not just her heart. "Artem…"

"I'm not going to force you to stay here. And I'm sure as hell not going to force myself on you. I'm leaving town for a few days, and I'd love nothing more than to find you here when I come back." He walked past her and grabbed a messenger bag from the table in the center of the room.

Ophelia couldn't believe what she was hearing. He'd taken her cat and lured her here, and now he was leaving? "You're *leaving*? Where are you going?"

"I'd rather not say. I've been called away for work, and I'll be back as soon as I can. The hotel staff has orders to provide whatever you need. You'll find them rather accommodating. Make yourself at home while I'm gone." His gaze flitted around the penthouse and paused, just for a moment, on the closed door to his home office. The room where he'd shut himself off on the morning she'd slipped away. "Take a look around."

Then he turned and walked right out the door.

Ophelia stared after him, dumbstruck. *This is insane.*

She walked to the bed and scooped Jewel into her arms, fully intending to give Artem a five-minute head start before going back downstairs and hailing a cab home.

She couldn't believe he actually expected her to stay here while he was gone. As if she could sleep in his bed, rest her head on his pillow, wake up every morning in his home and not wonder what it would be like to share it with him. Impossible. She couldn't do it.

"Come on, Jewel." She held the kitten closer to her heart. "Let's go home."

Home.

She blinked back tears. Damn Artem Drake. Damn him and his promises. *Let me take care of you.*

He was tender when she least expected it, and it messed with her head. As ridiculous as it seemed, she preferred it when he did things like break into her apartment and steal her cat.

She needed to get out of here. Now. She couldn't keep standing in his posh penthouse while the things he said kept spinning round and round in her head. She marched toward the door, but as she passed his office, her steps slowed.

Take a look around. What had that meant, anyway?

Nothing, probably.

She lingered outside the room, wanting to reach for the doorknob, even though she knew she shouldn't. She rolled her eyes. What could possibly be in there that would change her mind about anything?

Nothing. That's what.

He'd probably bought a crib. Or a bassinet. No doubt he thought she'd see it and go all mushy inside. Well, he was wrong. If he'd bought a crib—now, when she was only weeks pregnant—she'd know that the only reason he wanted to marry her was because of the baby. Giving the baby a proper, nuclear family was all he could think about. Just to prove it, if only to herself, she turned the knob and stepped inside his mysterious, secret room.

What she saw nearly made her faint again.

There was no crib. This wasn't a baby's room, and it most definitely wasn't an office. Ophelia's reflection stared back at her from all four of the mirrored walls. Beneath her feet was a smooth wood floor that smelled like freshly cut pine. A ballet barre stretched from one end of the room to the other.

Artem had built her a ballet studio, right here in his penthouse.

A lump formed in her throat. She couldn't swallow. She could barely even breathe.

Ophelia, you are *a dancer.*

He'd whispered those words before he knew about her illness, before he knew she was Natalia Baronova's granddaughter. She hadn't believed him then. Even as she'd danced across the moonlit floor of his living room, she'd doubted. She'd been performing a role, playing a part. That part had been the ballerina she'd been. The woman who could have done anything, been anything. A dancer. A mother. A wife. Once upon a time.

Ophelia, you are *a dancer.*

He'd really meant it. And now, standing in this room, she almost believed it, too.

Almost.

Chapter Fourteen

Artem was away longer than he'd planned. Three days, three nights. He'd hoped to take no more than an overnight trip, but things hadn't gone as smoothly as he'd anticipated. He hated being away and not knowing what was going on with Ophelia, but he'd been prepared to be gone as long as it took to set matters straight.

He returned to New York on the red-eye, hoping against hope he wasn't coming home to an empty penthouse. According to Dalton, Ophelia had been at work in the store on Fifth Avenue every day and seemed to be in perfectly good health. No fainting spells. No indication whatsoever that she was sick, or even pregnant. She hadn't missed a beat at work. But Artem had drawn the line at checking in with the staff at the Plaza to see whether or not she'd been staying in his suite. In truth, he hadn't been sure he wanted to know. Probably because he was almost certain she'd gone straight back to her own apartment after he'd left.

Sure enough, when he slipped inside the penthouse at 2:00 a.m.—quietly so as not to wake her, because a shred of optimism survived somewhere deep in his gut—the penthouse was empty. As was his bed.

Shit.

He let his messenger bag slide from his shoulder and land with a thud on the floor, its precious cargo forgotten. The air left his lungs in a weary rush. Until that moment, he hadn't realized he'd been all but holding his breath in anticipation as he'd flown clear across the continent.

He needed to see her. Touch her. Hold her. Three days was a damn long time.

He loosened his tie, crossed the room and collapsed on the bed. Eyes shut, surrounded by darkness, he could have sworn he caught Ophelia's sweet orchid scent on his pillow. The sheets felt sultry and warm. He must have been even more tired than he'd realized, because his empty bed didn't feel empty at all. He had to remind himself he was only being swallowed in sheets of memories.

But he could have sworn he heard the faint strains of music. Mozart's Piano Concerto no. 21. *La Petite Mort.* What was wrong with him? Clearly, he'd lost not only his Ophelia, but his mind, too.

You haven't lost her. Not yet.

There was still a ray of hope. A whisper of possibility. It was small, but he could feel it. He could see it in his mind's eye. It glittered like a gemstone.

Thud.

Out of nowhere, something landed on his chest, surprising him. He coughed and reached to push whatever it was off, and his hand made contact with something soft. And furry. And unmistakably feline.

He sat up and clicked on the light on the bedside table. Ophelia's tiny, white fluffball of a cat blinked up at him with wide, innocent eyes.

"Jewel. What are you doing here?" He gave the kitty a scratch on the side of her cheek and she leaned into it, purring furiously.

Artem had never been so happy to see an animal in his entire life. "Where's your mama, huh? Where's my Ophelia?"

My Ophelia.

There was no way she would have left the cat at his penthouse all alone. No possible way. She had to be here somewhere, but where?

He stood while Jewel settled onto his pillow, kneading her paws and purring like a freight train. At least someone was happy to see him.

The cat was in his apartment, though. That had to be a good sign.

"Ophelia?" His gaze swept the penthouse twice before he noticed a pale shaft of light coming from beneath his office door. Or what had *been* his office.

The ballet studio. Of course. He'd been so weary from the stress of the past few days that he'd almost forgotten he'd arranged a place for her to dance. Because she needed such a place, a room where she could let her body dream. If his trip had been a failure, if he could have given her only one thing, it would be the knowledge that she was perfect just as she was. Just as she'd always be. Ophelia would forever be a dancer. No illness, and certainly no man, could ever take that away from her.

He smiled to himself. The music hadn't been a product of wishful thinking, after all. Nor had it simply been a tender, aching memory. It was real, and it swelled as he approached the closed door, until the subtle strains of the violin exploded into a chorus of strings and piano notes that seemed to beat in time with the pounding of his heart.

He paused with his hand on the knob, remembering the last time he'd seen her dance to this music. He knew every moment, every movement by heart. He still dreamed about that dance every night, the whisper of her ballet shoes in the moonlight and the balletic bend of her spine when she'd arched against him as he'd entered her. Even his body remembered, perhaps more so than his mind. Because hearing that wrenching music and knowing Ophelia was right on the other side of the door, pointing her exquisite feet and arching her supple back, sent every drop of blood rushing straight to his groin. He was harder than he'd ever been in his life, hard as a diamond, and he'd yet to even set eyes on her.

With exaggerated slowness, he turned the knob and pushed the door open. The room was dark, the music loud. So loud she didn't notice his presence. She hadn't bothered to turn on the lights, and moonlight streamed through the skylights casting a luminescent glow on the smooth wood floors he'd had installed less than a week ago.

Ophelia stood at the barre with her back to him, wearing nothing more than her pink-ribboned pointe shoes and a sheer, diaphanous nightgown that ended just above her knees. In the soft light of the moon, Artem could see no more than a hint of her graceful spine and the curve of her ballerina bottom through the thin, delicate fabric. She rose up on tiptoe, reached her arm toward the center of the room, then bent toward the barre in an achingly glorious curve.

Seeing her like this, lost in her art, was like being inside a lucid dream. A lovely, forbidden fantasy. Part of him would have been happy to remain there in the doorway, a worshipful voyeur in the shadows. A sudden, fierce urge to inspect her body, with the thrill of knowing she was expecting his child, seized him. He took in the new softness of her frame, hips lush with femininity and a delicate voluptuousness that pierced his soul. But the other part of him—the demanding, lustful part that refused to be ignored—wanted to rip her gossamer gown away and bury himself inside her velvet soft warmth.

He prowled closer, footsteps swallowed by Mozart's tremulous melody. Artem didn't stop until he was close enough to feel the heat coming from her body, to see the dampness in the hair at the base of her swan-like neck. His fists clenched at his sides as he suppressed the overwhelming urge to touch her. Everywhere.

She turned on her tiptoes, and suddenly they were

face-to-face. Mouths, hearts, souls only inches apart. Artem would have given every cent he had for a sign— *any* sign—that she was happy to see him, that while he'd been gone she'd lain awake in his bed craving his hands on her body, dreaming of him bringing her to shattering climax with his mouth, his fingers, his cock.

"Artem." Her eyes were wide, her voice nothing but a breathy whisper, and for an agonizing moment, he thought she was on the verge of dancing away from him. As she'd done so many times.

But she didn't. She stayed put, breathing hard from exertion, breasts heaving with new fullness, her rose-petal nipples hardening beneath her whisper-thin gown. Pregnancy had changed her body in the most beautiful of ways, and knowing he'd been the one responsible for that divine transformation sent a surge of proprietary pride through him. The baby growing inside her was his. *She* was his, and he had every intention of showing her how profoundly that knowledge thrilled him.

She looked at him with eyes like flaming sapphires. And when the heat of her gaze dropped to his mouth with deliberate intent, it was all the invitation he needed.

"Kitten," he groaned, and pulled her to him, molding her graceful body to his.

His lips found hers in an instant, and the desperation that had been building in him in the weeks since he'd last tasted her reached its crescendo. He poured every bit of it into that kiss—all the fitful, restless nights, all the moments of the day when he'd thought of nothing but making love to her again. And again. And again.

They'd had one night together. He'd known it hadn't

been enough, but now he realized he'd never get his fill of her. If he lived a thousand years and spent every night buried in the sanctity of her precious body, he'd still want more.

Her hands found his hair and he deepened the kiss, trying to get closer to her. And closer still, until she let out a little squeak and he realized he'd pushed her up against the ballet barre.

Somehow he tore his mouth from hers long enough to gather her wisp of a nightie in his hands and lift it over her head. Then his lips found her again, this time at the base of her neck, where the erratic beat of her pulse told him how badly she'd wanted this, too. Needed it. Missed it. Missed *him*.

He cupped her breasts, lowered his head and kissed one nipple, then the other, drawing a deep moan of satisfaction from Ophelia's lips. She was so soft, so beautiful. Even more perfect than he remembered.

Time and again, he'd told himself that if he ever got to make love to her again, he'd go slow. He'd draw out each kiss, each caress, each lingering stroke as long as possible. He'd savor every heartbeat that led to their joining. But his blood boiled with need. He couldn't have slowed down if his life depended on it. And Ophelia matched his breathless hunger, sigh for sigh. She pulled at his hair, then clutched at his tie and wrapped it around her hand, holding him tightly to her as he drew her breast into his mouth, suckling. Savoring.

"Please, Artem," she begged. "Please."

"I'm here, kitten," he whispered against the soft

swell of her belly, where life—the life they'd created together—was growing inside.

He was here. And this time there would be no leaving. On either of their parts.

He unclenched her hands from his tie and placed each one on the ballet barre, curled them in place.

"I suggest you hold on," he murmured against her mouth, dipping his tongue inside and sliding it against hers for a final, searing kiss before dropping to his knees.

He slid his hands up and down the length of her gorgeous legs, parting her thighs. She had the legs of a dancer, legs that were made for moving to music and balancing on tiptoe. And for wrapping around his waist when he pushed himself inside her. But first, this. First the most intimate of kisses.

He devoured her like a starving man. And still he couldn't seem to get enough, even when she spread her ballerina thighs wider to give him fuller access. Somehow he grew only hungrier as she ground against him and her breathy little sighs grew louder and more urgent, rising with the music. He had to have her like this, wild and free and unafraid, forever.

Forever and always.

"Artem, I…" Her hands tightened in his hair with so much force that it bordered on pain, and he hummed against her parted flesh.

He wouldn't have stopped, even if she begged, even if she slid right down the wall into a puddle on the floor. Not until she found her release. Blood roared in his ears. If he hadn't been on his knees, his legs would have buckled beneath him. He was on the verge of coming himself and he'd yet to shed a single article of clothing.

Not yet.

He wanted her spent and trembling when he finally drove into her. He'd lived with the torture of wanting her for weeks, since he'd last touched her. They'd wasted so much time. Days. Weeks. Time when he'd fought his feelings for her and told himself what he'd done was wrong, when it couldn't have been more right.

Did she have any idea the kind of restraint it had taken not to act on his desire? To see her and pretend every cell in his body wasn't screaming to love her?

He needed her to know. He needed her to feel it with explosive force.

He moved his hands up the back of her quaking thighs, and the moment he dug his fingertips into the lush flesh of her bottom, she convulsed against him in rapturous release. And when she finally let herself go, the words on her lips were the ones Artem had waited a lifetime to hear.

"I love you."

Oh, my God.

Ophelia tightened her grip on the ballet barre as Artem rose to his feet and began to undress, his fiery gaze decisively linked with hers.

She was grateful for the barre, for the way it felt solid and familiar in her hands. She needed something real, something substantial to hold on to because this couldn't possibly be reality. This was too heavenly, too much like a beautifully choreographed dance—the kind that left you with a lump in your throat and tears running down your face at the end—to possibly be real.

She was naked and shivering and ravished, and she'd never felt more alive, more whole in her entire life. What had just happened? What had she just *said*?

I love you.

The words had slipped out before she could stop them, and now she'd never be able to take them back. Artem had certainly heard them—the Artem who stood in front of her, naked and hard now, more aroused than she would have thought humanly possible, plus the roomful of Artems reflected in the mirrored walls. He was everywhere. Here. Now. Surrounding her with his audacious, seductive masculinity.

She couldn't think, couldn't breathe, couldn't even figure out where to look. Her gaze flitted from the hard, chiseled planes of his abdomen to the mirror where she could see the sculpted sinews of his back and his firmly muscled backside. He was beautiful, like a god—the Apollo of Balanchine's *Orpheus*, an embodiment of poetry, music, dance and song, all the things she held most near and dear to her heart.

"Oh, kitten," he whispered, sliding a hand through her hair and resting his forehead against hers.

His erection pressed hot and wanting against her stomach, and in that perfect, precious moment he felt so big and capable that anything seemed possible. He was bigger than her fears. Bigger than her past. Bigger than her illness.

"I love you, too," he breathed, as he pushed inside her, pressing her into the barre. "I've loved you all along."

It was such ecstasy to have him filling her again, she could have wept. She'd been waiting for this since the morning she'd fled his penthouse. She just hadn't wanted to admit it. How could she have been so foolish to think she could live without this, without *him*, when the notion was impossible in every way? She rested her hands on his chest, wanting to imprint her touch there somehow, to mark him as hers, this magnificent man who refused to let her push him away.

At the moment of their joining, he groaned and she slid her hands down and around, reaching for his hips so she could anchor him in place. She wanted to hold on to this moment, this moment of coming together, while her entire body sighed in relief.

She could feel him throbbing and pulsing deep in her center, and it was almost too much. Too much pleasure. Too much sensation. She was going to come again. Soon. And he hadn't even moved.

"Do you have any idea how I've missed you?" he whispered into her hair, as he started to slide in and out. Slow at first, with languid, tender strokes as the pressure gathered and built, bearing down on her with frightening intensity.

"Yes," she whimpered. "I do... I do."

I do.

Wedding vows.

"My bride," he murmured, with aching sincerity in his voice as he thrust faster. Harder.

And she didn't fight it this time. Couldn't, even if she'd wanted to. Because since the moment she'd walked into this room, this mirrored place of hope, all her fractured pieces had somehow come together. She'd stayed at Artem's penthouse while he'd been gone. Because of this room. Every night, she found herself slipping on her ballet shoes and dancing again. Because of this room. She was healing. Because of this room.

She didn't feel like Ophelia Rose anymore—that sad, sick girl who'd given up on life. On dance. On love. Nor did she feel like Ophelia Baronova, because that Ophelia had known nothing but ballet. She'd never known how it felt to come apart in the arms of a man who loved her. She'd never lived with secret knowledge that life was growing inside her. A future. A real one.

A family.

No, she felt different now. Hopeful. Whole. The woman she felt like now was a dancer, a lover, a mother. And her name was Ophelia Drake.

"Tell me," Artem commanded, his eyes going sober, his strokes longer, deeper. She didn't think it was possible to love him more, but the deeper he pulsed inside her, the deeper she fell. "Look at me, kitten. I need to hear it. I love you with everything I have, everything I am. Tell me you'll be my wife."

"Yes," she whispered, unable to stop the tears from filling her eyes. "I will."

He kissed her with a tenderness so different from the violent climax building inside her that it felt like a dream. A beautiful, impossible dream.

"Don't be scared, baby," he murmured against her lips.

"I'm not." She clenched her inner muscles around

him, drawing a moan of pure male satisfaction from his soul. "Not anymore."

Then he was slamming into her with such delicious desperation that she could no longer keep her orgasm at bay. It tore through her and she cried out just as Artem pushed into her with a final mighty thrust. He shuddered and groaned his release as her back pressed harder against the ballet barre, and somehow she had the wherewithal to open her eyes so she could watch him climax. She wanted to see the perfection of his pleasure mirrored back at her, silvery reflections as plentiful and exquisite as the facets of a diamond.

They stayed that way, against the wall with their hearts crashing into each other, until their breathing slowed and the music went silent. Then, and only then, did Artem pull back to look at her. He brushed the hair from her eyes and covered her face with tender kisses.

I love you.

I love you.

I love you.

She wasn't sure if the words were hers or his. If they were merely thoughts or if one of them said them aloud. It had become like a heartbeat. Natural. Unstoppable.

Artem lowered his lips to her ear and whispered, "I think this occasion calls for a diamond. Don't you?"

Laugher bubbled up her throat. "Don't tell me you still have Princess Grace's necklace lying about?"

"No." He shook his head. His sensual lips were curved in a knowing grin, but the look in his eyes was pure seriousness. "Better."

She swallowed. Hard. "Better?"

Had he bought her an engagement ring? Was he about to reach into his suit pocket on the floor and retrieve one those infamous Drake-blue boxes with a white satin bow?

"Wait here," he ordered, his gaze flitting ever so briefly to her discarded nightgown pooled at her feet. "And don't even think about getting dressed."

She grinned as her heart pounded against her rib cage. "As you wish."

He blew her a kiss and strode naked out of the room, while she stared openly at his beautiful body. She could hardly believe this breathtaking man was going to be her husband. The father of her baby.

She slid her hands over her belly and marveled at the subtle, firm swell and the new heaviness in her breasts that meant Artem's child was growing inside her. It felt like a miracle. The doctor at the hospital had been right. Her breakout MS symptoms had all but gone away over the past few days. She felt healthier now, more herself, than she had since before her diagnosis. Some new mothers with MS experienced a relapse shortly after giving birth, but she wasn't worrying about that yet. She had the best doctors money could buy, and whatever happened, she could deal with it. Just like other new mothers did.

"You're beautiful, you know. More beautiful than I've ever seen you," Artem said, as he walked back into the studio holding a large black velvet box. Far too large for a simple engagement ring. "I have a mind to keep you barefoot and pregnant."

Ophelia laughed. "Are you forgetting I have a job

that I love? Besides, I'm not barefoot. There are ballet shoes on my feet."

She pointed a toe at him, and he grinned. "Even better, kitten. Be still my heart."

"What have you got there?" she asked, eyeing the velvet box. "Elizabeth Taylor's bracelet? Queen Elizabeth's tiara?"

"No," he said quietly. "Your grandmother's."

He lifted the lid of the box to reveal a glittering diamond tiara resting on a dark satin pillow. Eight delicate scrolls of tiny, inlaid diamonds curled up from the base, surrounding a stunning central stone. A yellow diamond. Just like…

"No." She started to tremble from head to toe. "This isn't…"

She couldn't even form the words. *The Drake Diamond.* It was too much to hope for. Too much to even dream.

"Yes, kitten." It is. He lifted the tiara from the box and placed it gingerly on her head. "The Drake Diamond has found its way home."

She caught a glimpse of her reflection in the mirror and nearly fainted again. The Drake Diamond was back. In New York. Reset in its original design. And she wasn't looking at it in a fancy glass case, but sitting on her very own head.

She bit her lip to keep from crying. "But I don't understand. How is this possible? I thought a buyer in Mexico City bought it at the auction."

Realization dawned slowly. Mexico City… Artem's urgent business trip. *Oh, my God.*

Artem shrugged. "I bought it back."

"Drake Diamonds bought it back? Just days after it was auctioned off?" She started to shake her head, but was afraid to move when a priceless stone was sitting atop her head.

"No." Artem's voice softened, almost as if he were imparting a secret. "*I* bought it back. Not Drake Diamonds."

"You? *Personally?*" It was too much to wrap her bejeweled head around. Did Artem have that kind of money? Did anyone?

"Yes, me. So not to worry. There won't be any more talk about resigning as CEO. It looks like I'll be working at Drake Diamonds for the rest of my life now." He let out a laugh. "With Dalton, actually. We've decided to share the role."

"I think that's perfect," she said through her tears. "But why? You didn't have to do this for me. It's too much."

She was crying in earnest now, unable to stop the flow of tears. She'd never expected this. She'd come to terms with the loss of the diamond. It had been hard, but she'd accepted it. She was pretty much an expert on loss now.

Not anymore, a tiny voice whispered inside. *Not anymore.*

Artem gathered her in his arms and pulled her against his solid chest. "Shh. Don't cry. Please don't cry. I wanted you to have it. I want you to wear that diamond tiara when you walk down the aisle to me on the day I make you my wife. You were right. It's not just a stone. It's a part of family history. Mine. Yours."

He raised her chin with a touch of his finger so her gaze met his. It seemed as if all the love in the world was shining back at her from the depths of his eyes. "And now ours."

Then he kissed away each and every one of her diamond tears.

* * * * *

*If you liked this story about finding love in
the glittering world of jewels and New York City,
don't miss the next two books in
the DRAKE DIAMONDS trilogy,
available April 2017 & July 2017
wherever Harlequin Special Edition books
and ebooks are sold.*

www.Harlequin.com

*Can't get enough romance? Keep reading for
a special preview of WILD HORSE SPRINGS,
the latest engrossing novel in
the* RANSOM CANYON *series
by* New York Times *bestselling author Jodi Thomas,
coming in February 2017 from HQN Books!*

CODY WINSLOW THUNDERED through the night on a half-wild horse that loved to run. The moon followed them, dancing along the edge of the canyon as they darted over winter buffalo grass that was stiff with frost.

The former Texas Ranger watched the dark outline of the earth where the land cracked open wide enough for a river to run at its base.

The canyon's edge seemed to snake closer, as if it were moving, crawling over the flat plains, daring Cody to challenge death. One missed step might take him and the horse over the rim and into the black hole. They'd tumble maybe a hundred feet down, barreling over jagged rocks and frozen juniper branches as sharp as spears. No horse or man would survive.

Only, tonight Cody wasn't worried. He needed to ride, to run, to feel adrenaline pumping in his veins, to know he was alive. He rode hoping to outrun his dark mood. The demons that were always in his mind were chasing him tonight. Daring him. Betting him to take one more risk…the one that would finally kill him.

"Run," he shouted to the midnight mare. Nothing would catch him here. Not on his land. Not over land his ancestors had hunted on for thousands of years.

Fought over. Died for and bled into. Apache blood, set-tler blood, Comanchero blood mixed in him as it did in this part of Texas. His family tree was a tumbleweed of every kind of tribe that ever crossed the plains.

If the horse fell and they went to their deaths, no one would find them for weeks on this far corner of his ranch. Even the canyon that snaked off the great Palo Duro had no name here. It wasn't beautiful like Ran-som Canyon, with layers of earth revealed in a rainbow of colors. Here the rocks were jagged, shooting out of the deep earthen walls from twenty feet in some places, almost like a thin shelf.

The petrified-wood formations along the floor of the canyon reminded Cody of snipers waiting, unseen but deadly. Cody felt numb, already dead inside, as he raced across a place with no name on a horse he called Midnight.

The horse's hooves tapped suddenly over a low place where water ran off the flat land and into the canyon. Frozen now. Silent. Deadly black ice. For a moment the tapping matched Cody's heartbeat, then both horse and rider seemed to realize the danger at once.

Cody leaned back, pulling the reins, hoping to stop the animal in time, but the horse reared in panic. Danc-ing on her hind legs for a moment before twisting vio-lently and bucking Cody off.

As Cody flew through the night air, he almost smiled. The battle he'd been fighting since he was shot and left for dead on the border three years ago was about to end here on his own land. The voices of all the ancestors who came before him whispered in the wind, as if calling him.

When he hit the frozen ground so hard it knocked the air from his lungs, he knew death wouldn't come easy tonight. Though he'd welcome the silence, Cody knew he'd fight to the end. He came from generations of fighters. He was the last of his line, and here in the dark he'd make his stand. Too far away to call for help. And too stubborn to ask, anyway.

As he fought to breathe, his body slid over a tiny river of frozen rain and into the black canyon.

He twisted, struggling to stop, but all he managed to do was tumble down. Branches whipped against him, and rocks punched his ribs with the force of a prize-fighter's blow. And still he rolled. Over and over. Ice on his skin, warm blood dripping into his eyes. He tried bracing for the hits that came when he landed for a moment before his body rolled again. He grabbed for a rock or a branch to hold on to, but his leather gloves couldn't get a grip on the ice.

He wasn't sure if he managed to relax or pass out, but when he landed on a flat rock near the bottom of the canyon, total blackness surrounded him and the few stars above offered no light. For a while he lay still, aware that he was breathing. A good sign. He hurt all over. More proof he was alive.

He'd been near death before. He knew that sometimes the body turned off the pain. Slowly, he mentally took inventory. There were parts that hurt like hell. Others he couldn't feel at all.

Cody swore as loud as he could and smiled. At least

he had his voice. Not that anyone would hear him in the canyon. Maybe his brain was mush; he obviously had a head wound. The blood kept dripping into his eyes. His left leg throbbed with each heartbeat and he couldn't draw a deep breath. He swore again.

He tried to move and pain skyrocketed, forcing him to concentrate to stop shaking. Fire shot up his leg and flowed straight to his heart. Cody took shallow breaths and tried to reason. He had to control his breathing. He had to stay awake or he'd freeze. He had to keep fighting. Survival was bone and blood to his nature.

The memory of his night in the mud near the Rio Grande came back as if it had been only a day ago, not three years. He'd been bleeding then, hurt, alone. Four rangers had stood on the bank at dusk. He'd seen the other three crumple when bullets fell like rain.

Only, it had been hot that night, so silent after all the gunfire. Cody had known that every ranger in the area would be looking for him at first light; he had to make it to dawn first. Stay alive. They'd find him.

But not this time.

No one would look for him tonight or tomorrow. No one would even notice he was gone. He'd made sure of that. He'd left all his friends back in Austin after the shooting. He'd broken up with his girlfriend, who'd said she couldn't deal with hospitals. When he came back to his family's land, he didn't bother to call any of his old friends. He'd grown accustomed to the solitude. He'd needed it to heal not just the wounds outside, but the ones deep inside.

Cody swore again.

The pain won out for a moment and his mind drifted. At the corners of his consciousness, he knew he needed to move, stop the bleeding, try not to freeze, but he'd become an expert at drifting that night on the border. Even when a rifle had poked into his chest as one of the drug runners tested to see if he was alive, Cody hadn't reacted.

If he had, another bullet would have gone into his body, which was already riddled with lead.

Cody recited the words he'd once had to scrub off the walls in grade school. Mrs. Presley had kept repeating as he worked, *Cody Winslow, you'll die cussing if you don't learn better.*

Turned out she might be right. Even with his eyes almost closed, the stars grew brighter and circled around him like drunken fireflies. If this was death's door, he planned to go through yelling.

The stars drew closer. Their light bounced off the black canyon walls as if they were sparks of echoes.

He stopped swearing as the lights began to talk.

"He's dead," one high, bossy voice said. "Look how shiny the blood is."

Tiny beams of light found his face, blinding him to all else.

A squeaky sound added, "I'm going to throw up. I can't look at blood."

"No, he's not dead," another argued. "His hand is twitching and if you throw up, Marjorie Martin, I'll tell Miss Adams."

All at once the lights were bouncing around him, high voices talking over each other.

"Yes, he is dead."

"Stop saying that."

"You stop saying anything."

"I'm going to throw up."

Cody opened his eyes. The lights were circling around him like a war party.

"See, I told you so."

One beam of light came closer, blinding him for a moment, and he blinked.

"He's hurt. I can see blood bubbling out of him in several spots." The bossy voice added, "Don't touch it, Marjorie. People bleeding have germs."

The gang of lights streamed along his body as if trying to torture him or drive him mad as the world kept changing from black to bright. It occurred to him that maybe he was being abducted by aliens, but he doubted the beings coming to conquer the world would land here in West Texas or that they'd sound like little girls.

"Hell," he said, and to his surprise the shadows all jumped back.

After a few seconds he made out the outline of what might be a little girl, or maybe ET.

"You shouldn't cuss, mister. We heard you way back in the canyon yelling out words I've seen written but never knew how to pronounce."

"Glad I could help with your education, kid. Any chance you have a cell phone or a leader?"

"We're not allowed to carry cell phones. It interferes with our communicating with nature." She shone her flashlight in his eyes. "Don't call me *kid*. Miss Adams says you should address people by their names. It's more polite. My name is Melanie Miller and I could read before I started kindergarten."

Cody mumbled a few words, deciding he was in hell already and, who knew, all the helpers' names started with *M*.

All at once the lights went jittery again and every one of the six little girls seemed to be talking at the same time.

One thought he was too bloody to live. One suggested they should cover him with their coats; another voted for undressing him. Two said they would never touch blood. One wanted to put a tourniquet around his neck.

Cody was starting to hope death might come faster when another shadow carrying a lantern moved into the mix. "Move back, girls. This man is hurt."

He couldn't see more than an outline, but the new arrival was definitely not a little girl. Tall, nicely shaped, hiking boots, a backpack on her back.

Closing his eyes and ignoring the little girls' constant questions, he listened as a calm voice used her cell to call for help. She had the location down to latitude and longitude and described a van parked in an open field about a hundred yards from her location where they could land a helicopter. When she hung up, she knelt at his side and shifted the backpack off her shoulder.

As she began to check his injuries, her voice calmly gave instructions. "Go back to the van, girls. Two at a time, take turns flashing your lights at the sky toward the North Star. The rest of you get under the blankets and stay warm. When you hear the chopper arrive, you can watch from the windows, but stay in the van.

"McKenna, you're in charge. I'll be back as soon as they come."

Another *M*, Cody thought, but didn't bother to ask.

To his surprise the gang of ponytails marched off like tiny little soldiers.

"How'd you find me?" Cody asked the first of a dozen questions bouncing around in his aching head as the woman laid out supplies from her pack.

"Your cussing echoed off the canyon wall for twenty miles." Her hands moved along his body, not in a caress, but to a man who hadn't felt a woman's touch in years, it wasn't far from it.

"Want to give me your name? Know what day it is? What year? Where you are?"

"I don't have brain damage," he snapped, then regretted moving his head. "My name's Winslow. I don't care what day it is or what year for that matter." He couldn't make out her face. "I'm on my own land. Or at least I was when my horse threw me."

She might have been pretty if she wasn't glaring at him. The lantern light offered that flashlight-to-the-chin kind of glow.

"Where does it hurt?" She kept her voice low, but she didn't sound friendly. "As soon as I pass you to the medics, I'll start looking for your horse. The animal might be out here, too, hurting or dead. Did he fall with you?"

Great! His Good Samaritan was worried more about the horse than him. "I don't know. I don't think so. When I fell off the edge of the canyon, Midnight was still standing, probably laughing at me." He took a breath as the woman moved to his legs. "I tumbled for what seemed like miles. It hurts all over."

"How did this happen?"

"The horse got spooked when we hit a patch of ice," he snapped again, tired of talking, needing all his strength to handle the pain. Cusswords flowed out with each breath. Not at her, but at his bad luck.

She ignored them as she brushed over the left leg of his jeans already stained dark with blood. He tried to keep from screaming. He fought her hand as she searched, examining, and he knew he couldn't take much more without passing out.

"Easy," she whispered as her blood-warmed fingers cupped his face. "Easy, cowboy. You've got a bad break. I have to do what I can to stabilize you and slow the blood flow. They'll be here soon. You've got to let me wrap a few of these wounds so you don't bleed out."

He nodded once, knowing she was right.

In the glow of the lantern she worked, making a tourniquet out of his belt, carefully wrapping his leg, then his head wound.

Her voice finally came low, sexy maybe if it were a different time, a different place. "It looks bad, but I don't see any chunks of brain poking out anywhere."

He didn't know if she was trying to be funny or just stating a fact. He didn't bother to laugh. She put a bandage on the gash along his throat. It wasn't deep, but it dripped a steady stream of blood.

As she wrapped the bandage, her breasts brushed against his cheek, distracting him. If this was her idea of doctoring a patient with no painkillers, it was working. For a few seconds there, he almost forgot to hurt.

"I don't have water to clean the wounds, but the dressing should keep anything else from getting in."

Cody began to calm. The pain was still there, but the demons in the corners of his mind were silent. Watching her move in the shadows relaxed him.

"Cody," he finally said. "My first name is Cody."

She smiled then for just a second.

"You a nurse?" he asked.

"No. I'm a park ranger. If you've no objection, I'd like to examine your chest next."

Cody didn't move as she unzipped his jacket. "I used to be a ranger, but I never stepped foot in a park." He could feel her unbuttoning his shirt. Her hand moved in, gently gliding across his ribs.

When he gasped for air, she hesitated, then whispered, "One broken rib." A moment later she added, "Two."

He forced slow, long breaths as he felt the cold night air pressing against his bare chest. Her hand crossed over his bruised skin, stopping at the scars he'd collected that night at the Rio Grande.

She lifted the light. "Bullet wounds?" she questioned more to herself than him. "You've been hurt bad before."

"Yeah," he said as he took back control of his mind and made light of a gunfight that almost ended his life. "I was fighting outlaws along the Rio Grande. I swear it seemed like that night almost two hundred years ago. Back when Captain Hays ordered his men to cross the river with guns blazing. We went across just like that, only chasing drug runners and not cattle rustlers like they did back then. But we were breaking the law not to cross just the same."

He closed his eyes and saw his three friends. They'd gone through training together and were as close as brothers. They wanted to fight for right. They thought they were invincible that night on the border, just like Captain Hays's men must have believed.

Only, those rangers had won the battle. They'd all returned to Texas. Cody had carried his best friend back across the water that night three years ago, but Hobbs hadn't made it. He'd died in the mud a few feet from Cody. Fletcher took two bullets but helped Gomez back across. Both men died.

"I've heard of that story about the famous Captain Hays." She brought him back from a battle that had haunted him every night for three years. "Legend is that not one ranger died that night. They rode across the Rio screaming and firing. The bandits thought there were a hundred of them coming. But, cowboy, if you rode with Hays, that'd make you a ghost tonight and you feel like flesh and blood to me. Today's rangers are not allowed to cross."

Her hand was moving over his chest lightly, caressing now, calming him, letting him know that she was near. He relaxed and wished they were somewhere warm.

"You're going to make it, Winslow. I have a feeling you're too tough to die easy."

Don't miss WILD HORSE SPRINGS by
New York Times *bestselling author Jodi Thomas,*
available February 2017 wherever
HQN books and ebooks are sold!

www.Harlequin.com

Wrapped more tightly in the shawl, she clomped across the wooden porch, the sound then muffled in the dirt as she made her way past the paddock to the foreman's cabin. The clear, starry night was silent and still, save for the thrum of crickets' chirping, the distant howl of a coyote. The cabin's front door swung open before she reached Colin's porch, a spear of light guiding her way. And with that, the full ramifications of what she was doing—or about to do, anyway—slammed into her.

But she had no idea what it might mean to Colin, she thought as his broad-shouldered silhouette filled the doorway, fragmenting the light. Maybe nothing, really— oh, hell, her heart was about to pound right out of her chest—since men were much more adept at these things than women. Weren't they?

Spudsy scampered out onto the porch from behind Colin's feet, wriggling up a storm when he saw her, and Emily's heart stopped its whomping long enough to squeeze at the sight of the bundle of furry joy she'd come to love.

At least she'd be able to keep the dog, she thought as she scooped up the little puppy to bury her face in his ruff, trying to ignore Colin's piercing gaze.

Oh, hell. That whole "sex as fun" thing? Who was she kidding? That wasn't her. Never had been. What on earth had made her think a single event would change *her*?

Although this one just might.

"I made a fire," Colin said quietly. Carefully. As though afraid she might spook. Never mind this had been her idea.

"That's nice."

Ergh.

Something like a smile ghosted around his mouth. "We can always just talk. No expectations. Isn't that what you said?" He shoved his hands into his pockets. "You're safe, honey. With me." His lips curved. "*From me.*"

Still cuddling the puppy, she came up onto the porch. Closer. Too close. But not so close that she couldn't, if she were so inclined, still grab common sense by the hand and run like hell.

"And from myself?"

"That, I can't help you with."

Another step closer. Then another, each one a little farther away from common sense, whimpering in the dust behind her. "Kiss me," she whispered.

Don't miss
FALLING FOR THE REBOUND BRIDE
by Karen Templeton,
available February 2017 wherever
Harlequin® Special Edition books and ebooks are sold.

www.Harlequin.com

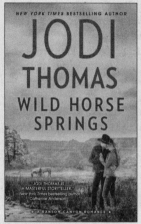